D0063918

Journeyman

Journeyman

ERSKINE CALDWELL

Foreword by Edwin T. Arnold

BROWN THRASHER BOOKS

THE UNIVERSITY OF GEORGIA PRESS

ATHENS AND LONDON

Published in 1996 as a Brown Thrasher Book
by the University of Georgia Press, Athens, Georgia 30602
© 1935, 1963 by Erskine Caldwell
Foreword to the Brown Thrasher Edition © 1996
by the University of Georgia Press

The paper in this book meets the guidelines for permanence and
durability of the Committee on Production Guidelines for
Book Longevity of the Council on Library Resources.

Printed in the United States of America

oo 99 98 97 96 P 5 4 3 2 1

Library of Congress Cataloging in Publication Data

Caldwell, Erskine, 1903–
Journeyman / Erskine Caldwell ; foreword by Edwin T. Arnold.
p.   cm.
"Brown Thrasher books."
ISBN 0–8203–1848–5 (pbk. : alk. paper)
1. Fundamentalism—Southern States—Fiction. 2. Evangelicalism—
Southern States—Fiction. 3. Depressions— Southern States—Fiction. I. Title
PS3505.A322J7   1996
813'.52—dc20   96–4267

British Library Cataloging in Publication Data available

First published in a limited edition by the Viking Press.

FOR LEGARDE DOUGHTY

Foreword

Edwin T. Arnold

BETWEEN 1931 and 1935, Erskine Caldwell wrote three novels. Two earned him both wealth and fame. *Tobacco Road* (1932) and *God's Little Acre* (1933) became controversial best sellers and today form the heart of his critical reputation. The third book, the largely forgotten *Journeyman* (1935), bedeviled him during the writing, confounded him during publication, and initially cost him money and critical standing. Five years passed before Caldwell published another novel, an indication of the toll *Journeyman* took on him. Yet now it seems one of his finest fictional works, a surprisingly complex and sophisticated study of fundamentalist evangelical religion in the depression–era South. No other novel shows so clearly Caldwell's roots in Old Southwest humor and lore; and, before his publication of *Deep South* in 1968, no other work revealed so thoroughly his equivocal attitudes toward the role of faith and dogma in rural society.[1]

Caldwell began writing *Journeyman* in early 1933, while awaiting the publication of *God's Little Acre* by Viking Press.[2] He set it aside in May while he worked as a screenwriter for MGM, first on location in Louisiana and then in Hollywood. During this time he also selected the stories for his second collection, *We Are the Living*, which Viking would publish in early Fall. Upon his return to his home in Mount Vernon, Maine, in August, he made final revisions to *Journeyman*, guided by his first wife Helen's crucial critical judgment, and then submitted the manuscript to his editor Marshall Best in September. Viking had been anxious to follow *God's Little Acre* with another novel, but *Journeyman* was a disappointment to them. They did not consider it an advance over his earlier fiction, and they encouraged Caldwell to "put the book aside or at least rework it."[3] They were, moreover, concerned that the book would embroil them in yet more censorship battles of the sort they were already fighting for Caldwell, and they were uncertain that they could defend *Journeyman* on its artistic merits as they were *God's Little Acre*. Caldwell, never certain of the quality of his work, was shaken by Viking's reluctance. "I wish to god I knew about the book," he wrote Helen in November. "If I *knew* it was good, I'd let it be published. I think it is, and I feel it is, but how can you be sure."[4]

In the meantime, Caldwell's agent, Maxim Lieber, was taking advantage of Viking's reluctance. He entered discussions with publishers Harcourt Brace, Random House, and Covice–Friede, all of whom were interested in buying Caldwell and the book away from Viking. Based on this interest, Caldwell "politely told Viking to go to hell": "I could not reason out why I should let Viking publish the novel when they didn't like it, and at the same time when another publisher [Harcourt Brace] was anxious to hand out that much money [two thousand dollars] even before he read the book," he wrote to his friend Alfred Morang.[5] But once these parties had actually examined the manuscript, their reactions were similar to Viking's, and all three eventually withdrew their offers. Lieber nevertheless tried to pressure Viking into publishing the book, using these negotiations as leverage, but Viking remained unmoved and even encouraged Lieber to make any outside deal he could. Their best offer was to advance Caldwell one thousand dollars on the book but to withhold publication until Caldwell had written and published another novel, judged superior in quality to *Journeyman*.[6] Thus, Caldwell was stuck, and for a year the book sat, a source of continued anxiety and concern to the author.

On December 4, 1933, Jack Kirkland's play version of *Tobacco Road* opened at the Masque Theater in New York City; in January it moved to the 48th Street Theater and settled in for its record–breaking run of seven and a half years, a total of 3,180 performances. In May 1934, Caldwell wrote an angry four–part series for the *Daily Worker* on the automobile industry in Detroit. In June he returned to Hollywood for a two month stint at MGM. Driving back across the country in August, he gathered material for a proposed "Cross–America" series. Thus, it eventually became clear to Viking that their author, whose reputation continued to grow, would not soon present them with another novel. Finally, publisher Harold Guinzburg agreed to issue *Journeyman*— either in a standard trade edition if Caldwell would revise it, or, if Caldwell refused, in a limited edition of 1,475 copies, signed by the author. Such a compromise would give Caldwell his publication but would, Guinzburg hoped, protect the company and circumvent the censors. Caldwell felt trapped. If he did not agree to the limited publication, Viking would not defend the book in court. At the same time, he did not want to self–censor his own work. "What the hell can I do?" he wrote Morang in October 1934. "Yes or no. A publisher has got you, no matter which way you turn." A few days later he wrote Morang again, "I told them to go to hell before I'd change it, and I don't know what is going to be done."[7]

The limited edition was published in January 1935, and the reviews were, as feared, mostly negative. Many critics felt that Caldwell was simply repeating himself, mining the same southern subjects, indulging in gratuitous sexuality and violence while this time adding religious blasphemy for good measure. In the words of James T. Farrell, "If this story be taken simply as a fantastic burlesque, it is passably humorous and diverting. However, if it is to be considered as a serious novel, purporting to reveal an understanding of a section of the American scene and intending to give us an awareness and a sense of the people in this milieu, an estimation of the novel becomes a different question. It is difficult to note any underlying theme. Rather, *Journeyman* seems to be just another story hastily rolled off Caldwell's typewriter."[8] Thus, Viking's concerns appeared in all ways justified.

Three years later, however, Viking was ready to reconsider. The continued success of the play version of *Tobacco Road* led Caldwell to undertake and invest in a dramatization of *Journeyman* starring Will Geer as the preacher Semon Dye; and Viking, hoping to capitalize on the play, issued a trade edition of the novel in 1938. This time Caldwell agreed to revise the book, to remove the more controversial parts and to tone down the dialogue in order to have it in general release. But neither the play nor the revised book proved successful. In 1947 Penguin published the novel in paperback, and in those heady post–war years it sold over 750,000 copies, earning Caldwell money for the first time.[9] In 1950 it was again reprinted in hardback, with Caldwell's introduction, by Little, Brown in an arrangement with Duell, Sloan & Pearce, the company Caldwell moved to after leaving Viking. Thereafter, the book would appear mostly in paperback format, one in a long line of cheaply produced volumes with lurid and indistinguishable covers.

In retrospect, *Journeyman* seems a natural extension of the themes Caldwell explored in *Tobacco Road* and *God's Little Acre*—themes that illustrate, largely through negative examples, the fragility of social order and human dignity. Yet, for all of the degradation found in those novels, both Jeeter Lester and Ty Ty Walden maintain a belief in and even a companionable relationship with God. Clearly these partnerships are often comic and self–serving. Both men interpret God to suit themselves, just as does Sister Bessie in *Tobacco Road*, who constantly instructs God, especially on feminine matters that she assumes are foreign to Him. Nevertheless, Caldwell is unusually gentle in his depictions. Rather than stressing the religious hypocrisy of his characters, which from one perspective is truly great, he chooses to portray the essential, earnest aspect of their beliefs. Indeed, as others have noted, in these works Caldwell's characters expand the mystery of religion to include the animal and physical as well as the spiritual. Which is not to say that the Lesters or the Waldens are somehow rewarded by a benevolent Lord for their faith; it is impossible to avoid the terrific irony in the conclusion of each work. But it is equally difficult, and dangerously condescending, to condemn these people for holding on to whatever beliefs they have, given the stark realities of their lives.

In *Journeyman*, Caldwell places religion at center stage. As a boy and young man, he accompanied his father, the Reverend Ira Sylvester Caldwell, to many types of fundamentalist worship. I. S. Caldwell was a social liberal, hopeful that the poor could be rescued from their degraded economic and spiritual state through education and hygiene, or, more desperate, through eugenic control. He despaired over the power of "bogus religionists" who stirred their congregations into fits of frenzy while pursuing their own selfish, morally suspect agendas.[10] Erskine

Caldwell's first published work, an essay entitled "Georgia Cracker" (1926) written while a student at the University of Virginia, condemned "Holy Rollers, Snake Charmers, and the like" and gave a powerful description of one such religious service that anticipated the lengthy, brilliantly realized revival meeting at the conclusion of *Journeyman*.[11]

Although himself an avowed agnostic, Caldwell remained throughout his life a serious and largely respectful student of southern religion. *Journeyman* illustrates Caldwell's conflicting attitudes about the uses and misuses of religion, and the traveling preacher Semon Dye remains one of his most complex characterizations. In his 1950 introduction to the novel, Caldwell wrote, "In the beginning I had no inkling of what turn the story of Semon Dye in *Journeyman* would eventually take, but I had written only a few chapters when I became convinced that, come what would, I was bound to go along with him to the end. I am glad now that I did, even though there were times when I regretted ever having thought of the man, because when the novel was finished, I felt the satisfaction of having put on paper something of the evasive and tantalizing character of a human being often glimpsed but never before seen face to face."[12] Semon Dye is indeed tantalizing, for he is, in Caldwell's depiction, the devil himself, dropped into the aptly named hamlet of Rocky Comfort, Georgia, in a cloud of smoke, a demonic flatulence. However, he introduces himself to Clay Horey as a "man of God": "The Lord don't have to bother about me. He sort of gives me a free rein," Semon says. This boast establishes the comedy and the ambiguity of the novel.

Caldwell always spoke of Semon Dye (one of his finest names, in a book rich with symbolism and allusion) as a scoundrel. "He's an expert at winning souls, but I suppose you could win souls for the devil as well as for God," he explained in 1986.[13] But in the novel Caldwell shows remarkable understanding and compassion for both the victims of Semon's duplicity and for Semon himself. "The trouble was that Clay Horey and Tom Rhodes and Dene and Lorene, perhaps being no better or no worse than most of us, recognized Semon Dye as being exactly what he was but were powerless to cast off the spell he had put upon them," Caldwell wrote in his 1950 introduction. "They reproved him and they damned him, yet eagerly became the slaves of his will. And in the end they knew full well that they had been victimized by a rogue, but none the less they were sorry to see him leave."[14] In the novel Semon apparently falls as deeply under his own spell as does his congregation. It can, in fact, be argued that Semon truthfully sees himself as God's tool, as he may well be; and for all of the rowdy, carnal comedy in the book, Caldwell never actually dismisses the *results* of the preaching. Despite—or because of—all their failings, the people of Rocky Comfort do have spiritual yearnings, which they express by looking through a crack in a cow shed at the quiet woods beyond or by rolling on the ground in holy sexual ecstasy. When Semon leaves, they rightfully regret his passing, for he has helped them for a brief moment to touch their divinity, to "come through." At the same time, Caldwell suggests that during his stay in Rocky Comfort, Semon might have glimpsed something hidden in his own nature, that the man of sin may also have elements of the man of sorrow, and that his journey may yet be one of further discovery.

This novel will itself be a discovery to most readers. In this publication, the University of Georgia Press reprints Caldwell's original version, the text of the 1935 uncensored limited edition. This version of *Journeyman* is perhaps his finest extended tall tale, highly allusive and filled with energy and imbued with the extravagant vision and the moral subtext that is found in the truest of the traditional folklore from which it derives. Seen at the time as a disappointing follow–up to *Tobacco Road* and *God's Little Acre*, today *Journeyman* rightfully takes its place with those two novels as representing Caldwell at the height of his distinct and often extraordinary creativity.

NOTES

1. The book was first published in England under the title *In the Shadow of the Steeple* in 1966 (Heinemann); in America it was retitled *Deep South: Memory and Observation* (New York: Weybright & Talley, 1968).

2. In *Call It Experience*, Caldwell remembers beginning *Journeyman* in early 1934. However, as Harvey L. Klevar documents in his biography *Erskine Caldwell* ([Knoxville: University of Tennessee Press, 1993], 142–47), he actually began writing it the year before and submitted the manuscript to his editor Marshall Best in September 1933. See also Dan B. Miller, *Erskine Caldwell: The Journey from Tobacco Road* (New York: Knopf, 1995), 203–4. Miller is less specific in his description of the book's composition but gives the impression that it was finished in early 1934. Note that Miller misdates a letter from Caldwell to his wife Helen in constructing this chronology.

3. Miller, 204. Miller dates this letter from Marshall Best to Caldwell's agent Maxim Leiber as 15 October 1934, although evidence suggests 1933 as the more likely year.

4. Caldwell to Helen Caldwell, 18 November 1933, © 1996 by Virginia Caldwell Hibbs, Erskine Caldwell Collection, Baker Library, Dartmouth College, Hanover, N.H.

5. Caldwell to Alfred Morang, 29 October 1933, the Alfred Morang Papers, bMS Am 1638, reprinted by permission of the Houghton Library, Harvard

University, Harvard, Mass.; reprinted in Klevar, 143. Klevar mistakenly gives the amount as two hundred dollars.

6. Caldwell explained the situation in a letter to Helen Caldwell, 19 November 1933, © 1996 by Virginia Caldwell Hibbs, Erskine Caldwell Collection, Baker Library, Dartmouth College, Hanover, N.H. Caldwell worried that if he accepted Viking's offer, he would be unable to write another novel with *Journeyman* in limbo.

7. Miller, 204. The first letter is dated 17 October 1934; the second 24 October 1934. Miller conflates the two texts.

8. "Heavenly Visitation," *New Masses* 15 (April 2, 1935): 32–33; reprinted in *Critical Essays on Erskine Caldwell*, ed. Scott MacDonald (Boston: G. K. Hall & Co., 1981), 41.

9. See Miller, 328–36, for discussion of Caldwell's paperback publications.

10. See Miller, 122 27, for a description of Ira Caldwell's writings and views on these matters. See also Caldwell's meditation on his father and religion in *Deep South*, in which he describes some of the more eccentric services he witnessed.

11. See Miller, 79–81.

12. "Introduction" to *Journeyman* (Duell, Sloan & Pearce, 1950); reprinted in MacDonald, *Critical Essays*, 229–30.

13. Edwin T. Arnold, "Interview with Erskine Caldwell," in *Conversations with Erskine Caldwell*, ed. Edwin T. Arnold (Jackson: University Press of Mississippi, 1988), 281.

14. MacDonald, 229.

JOURNEYMAN

Chapter I

~~~

THE mud-spattered rattle-trap of an automobile rolled off the road and came to a dead stop beside the magnolia tree. The tall gaunt-looking man who looked as if he had been living on half-rations since the day he was weaned sat grim and motionless, with his hands gripped around the steeringwheel. His eyes were fastened upon the row of sagging fence posts ahead.

Clay Horey leaned forward in his chair on the porch, screwing up his eyes to soften the glare of the sun on white sand, and tried to see who was there. For a while he could not make himself believe that he had actually seen anyone there. Sitting on the porch staring at the colorless dry country, week after week, year after year, he had got so he could not believe his own eyes sometimes.

"That doggone old chicory just clouds up a man's eyes in the summertime," he said. "I ought to be getting me a jug of corn some of these days. Looks like there aint nothing else fit to shake a man awake."

With his eyes closed, Clay tried to hear through the ringing of heat in his ears the disturbance of a stranger's arrival. He

~~~

could recognize the jabbering of a jaybird and the screech of a tightening plowshare, and all the other familiar sounds that came to him from miles around over the sandy plowlands, but it was hard for him to distinguish strange sounds in his own front yard.

"It can't be so doggone much of anybody," he said at last, opening his eyes wide. "If it is, he's way off his track, coming out here."

Clay continued to stare at the grim-looking man in the topless car, shaking his head bewilderedly. He could think of no man in the whole world who would come from that direction, and at that time of day, to see him. He had no money to buy anything with, and he had no money to pay on what he owed; it was just a waste of time for anybody to go to the bother of coming so far out of the way to see him.

Once more he strained his eyes to see, but there was no motion within sight to convince him that he was not dreaming over the pot of chicory he had drunk for breakfast that morning. There were no clouds in the pale blue sky, there was no breeze to stir the leaves on the magnolia tree, there was no motion in the endless gliding and wheeling of the buzzards overhead, and now the ramshackle automobile and dust-stained stranger were as inert as the row of sagging fence posts beside the road.

Clay tried once more to convince himself that what he thought he had seen was merely an illusion of heat and sand. He would have liked to pull his hat down over his eyes and take another short little snooze before suppertime, but when he tried it, the mirage refused to be swept away merely by the motion of pulling down the brim of his hat. He sat up, angry and nervous, and stared across the yard.

"It couldn't be so doggone much of anybody," he said, "or he wouldn't have shut off the engine before he turned in off the road. I never did see anybody that pinched the gas tank who was worth a doggone."

Nearly five minutes had passed when the motor suddenly started to run backward of its own accord. The dust-stained man in the car jumped, and sat stiff and erect, appearing as if he had been waiting for it to happen but had been caught off guard.

The backward-running engine began going faster and faster. When a car that has been driven in the heat without water in the radiator, and with not much oil in the crankcase, begins to wind up backward of its own accord after the switch has been turned off, a man never has to wait long to find out what is going to happen. When it sounded to Clay as though the whole machine would break down under the grinding vibration that shook it from fender to fender, the motor suddenly unwound itself with a whirr like the breaking of the mainspring in an alarm clock. It ended with an ear-splitting backfire in the shattered exhaust pipe.

When it was all over, the stranger relaxed. A dense cloud of nauseating black smoke billowed over the car for a moment and then floated towards the house.

The echo of the backfire had barely died out when a bevy of bluejays swept out of the woods in a flurry, chattering and hawking as if they had discovered a snake in a tree.

"I reckon I ought to go ask him what he wants," Clay said.

"It looks like he aint got the sense to come in out of the heat of the day."

The wave of black smoke was beginning to disintegrate in the hot midday air, but the sickening odor hovered over the porch and began to drift through the open doors and windows of the house.

Clay jumped to his feet, upsetting his chair.

"Damn the man who'd drive right spang up to the front door and let loose a stink like that!" he said, wide awake at last. He began to feel sick in the pit of his stomach. "I've never been so doggone mad in all my life!"

He could bear it no longer. He leaned over the porch railing, pressing a thumb and forefinger against the sides of his nose, and blew with all his might. Even then he could still smell it; it was all the more sickening.

"Damn the man who'd do that right in the front yard," he said, shouting angrily at the tall leather-faced stranger.

Clay began beating against the post that held up the roof. He made so much noise, shaking the house with his hammering fists, that his wife came running through the hall to the door behind him.

"Who made that awful smell out here, Clay?" Dene asked haltingly. "It's the nastiest thing."

Clay pointed at the man getting out of the automobile under the magnolia tree.

Dene muttered something he could not understand and, holding her skirts to her knees, ran from the porch in wild-eyed fright.

Clay went down the steps into the yard. The man had got out and he was walking up and down in long strides, stretching his legs and stopping every few steps to shake one of his feet. The man's clothes were wrinkled and dust-stained. His leather-skinned face looked as if it had been sprayed with brown paint.

"My name's Semon Dye," he said, eying Clay from head to toe, but ignoring him as if he had been a stick of wood. "What's yours?"

He thrust out his hand at Clay, pushing it at him as though it were a pole wrapped in an old coat. Clay looked down at the hand, stepping back each time it was thrust closer. The hand followed him to the fence.

"I told you my name," Semon said. "Now, what's yours?"

Clay, his back against the fence post, looked at the big hand with its thumb sticking up like a nubbin of red corn.

"Me?" Clay said. "Why, I'm Clay Horey."

Semon seized his hand and shook it until Clay's arm felt numb.

"I'm mighty pleased to know you," Semon said, still shaking his hand. "I sure am pleased."

Semon dropped the hand, and it fell against Clay's thigh like a bag of buckshot.

Semon looked at the house and barn over Clay's shoulders, twisting his neck in order to see everything in sight.

"Nice-looking place you've got here," he said finally. "I used to own a fine farm myself, once."

He turned around and looked down the road towards the group of Negro cabins several hundred yards away. In front of the cabins stretched the cotton fields; behind them were the woods bordering the creek. Semon continued to look at the cabins.

"Hands?" he asked, opening his eyes wide and nodding his head slowly while he watched Clay's lips.

Clay nodded, following the motions of Semon's head, but catching himself in time to keep from opening his eyes as Semon did.

"Hardy and George are raising a little corn for me this year," Clay said. "They're out in the field somewhere now."

Semon turned once more and looked at the quarters. Clay followed his gaze, but he could see nothing down there to hold anybody's attention as it did Semon's.

While they waited and looked, a Negro girl came out of one of the cabins and went down the road.

Clay was still waiting for Semon Dye to state the nature of his business and to explain what he was doing out there. He was not accustomed to having strangers drive up and stop at his house, because the State road was eight or nine miles away, and the country road in front of the house led nowhere. It came to an end three miles up the creek in the middle of a canebrake.

Semon still did not offer to say what he was doing back there in the country.

"You're a long way from home, aint you?" Clay asked at last, unable to wait any longer.

"Yes and no," Semon said. "I am and I aint."

Semon jabbed his stiff thumb into Clay's left ribs, at the same time making a sucking sound with his lips that sounded as if he were calling a dog.

"Good God Almighty, man!" Clay shouted, jumping a foot into the air. "Don't never do that!"

"Ticklish?" Semon asked.

Clay regarded him carefully from the corner of his eye.

"No," he said, "but I just never could stand to be goosed."

"Some folks are like that," Semon said. "I reckon you must be one of them."

"That's how I figured it," Clay said, scowling, and rubbing his ribs. "I never thought I'd have to be told about it, though."

Semon laughed for the first time, and started to the house. He did not wait for Clay.

"It feels pretty good to be here, after riding like I have," Semon said. "The best part of it is in getting here in plenty of time for supper."

They were half way to the house. Clay ran up behind Semon and grabbed him by the coat tail.

"Now, wait a minute," Clay said threateningly, jerking Semon's coat excitedly. "Now, just hold on here a minute."

Semon shook him loose with a tug of his coat.

"Don't you dare lay hands on a man of God, Horey," he said sternly.

Clay stared up at the leather-colored face.

"You wouldn't happen to be a preacher, would you?" he asked, atremble, seeing for the first time the black dust-stained suit and hat and the stringy black bow tie.

"I am, I am," Semon stated, his brows dropping to a straight line across his face. "Don't you lay hands on a man of God, Horey. I am Semon Dye."

He reached forward to jab Clay with his stiff thumb, but Clay jumped beyond his reach.

"Well, then, that's all the difference in the world," Clay said, going ahead and leading the way to the porch. "That makes one hell of a difference, since you're Semon Dye. I did hear the name out there under the tree, but I didn't pay a bit of attention to it. I sure am glad you reminded me of it, too. I somehow got the notion in my head that you was a good-for-nothing rascal out for no good. But that makes all the difference in the world between me and you. You are as welcome as the day is long. I sure feel proud to have you. I sure do, even if I do say it myself."

Semon looked down upon him from his great height, smiling and nodding his head to show that he held no hard feelings.

"I'm mighty proud to see you come," Clay said. "Aiming to do some preaching around here somewhere?"

"Nothing else but," Semon said. He stopped and looked down the road again towards the Negro cabins. The girl had gone out of sight in a bend of the road. "Reckon you could fix me up for a spell, coz?"

"I'll do my doggone best," Clay said. "However, it's true that I aint got much. Not much more'n you see right now."

"That's all right," Semon said, laying a hand on Clay's shoulders. "I aint used to a splurge, anyway, except when it comes to having a little fun with the girls and women. When a man feels the need of a little poontang to perk him up, he feels like making short shift with what satisfies ordinary people."

"Well," Clay said, "I don't know that I ought to say it, but——"

"Don't mistake me for kicking yet, coz," Semon said, patting his shoulder. "I've hardly had a chance to do any looking around so far."

"Well, it's just like I started out to say," Clay put in. "Maybe this aint exactly the place you aimed for, because to tell the truth——"

"Don't let that worry you, Horey. If I can't get the lay of the land by tomorrow morning, I'll just pack up and move on. I've been traveling and preaching almost all my life, and I can make hay where the next man can't see nothing but stony ground."

Clay shook his head, but pulled up a chair for Semon to sit down in.

"It's going to be pretty rough-going here," Clay said after thinking a while. "There hasn't been a preacher of count around here in I don't know how many years, maybe not for eight or ten of them. The last one I recall about said he did his damnedest, but it wasn't no use. He said when he left that the folks had gone too far to help any in this life."

"The sinfuller they are, the better I like it," Semon said, putting his feet on the railing and leaning back in the chair. "I came here to preach the wickedness out of you people, and what I start, I finish."

"You've got a pretty big order on your hands then. You don't know the people in Rocky Comfort like I do. I was born among them, and I'm still one of them. When it comes to being sinful, I don't know nobody else in Georgia that's in the running. That's God's own truth, if I do say it."

"That's because they've never had the voice of Semon Dye to scare the daylights out of their sinful natures," he said, shaking his head. "I've never had a single complaint in all my days of preaching. People all over say I sure know how to get the Devil's number, and I'll run the Devil out of this place, if I don't drop dead before I'm done."

Clay glanced at Semon's big hands and feet, and at the six feet and eight inches of him that had bent double in the middle when he propped his feet on the railing.

"I don't need preaching to as bad as some of the rest of them," Clay told him. "I'm proud to say that. I've been leading a right straight life for the past seven or eight months, or more. I've never been so doggone good in all my days before. I don't know what gets into me, at times. I just don't ache to be bad no more. I'd a heap rather sit here on my porch, through the spring and summer, than to go out and be bad."

"Everybody's wicked," Semon stated grimly.

"Everybody?" Clay asked, hesitating a moment. "You too?"

Semon laughed a little, turning towards Clay as though he was about to jab him in the ribs again. Clay moved his chair a few more inches.

"I'm Semon Dye," he said, suddenly becoming stern. "The Lord don't have to bother about me. He sort of gives me a free rein."

"I reckon that would come in handy at times," Clay said.

"Coz," Semon said, winking one of the slits in his leather-tight face, "you spoke a mouthful."

There was a noise of some kind just inside one of the windows. Both Semon and Clay turned around when they heard it.

"You don't live here all by yourself, do you, Horey?" he said.

"Not so you could notice it. I've got a wife inside the house, there. I reckon that was her making that noise we just heard. She's awful curious about strangers, but it's like dragging an ox by the tail to try to make her be sociable with somebody she never saw hair of before. We've been married now only since last fall. Dene's daddy took sick and died last November, and he didn't stay dead three days before me and her got married."

Semon nodded approvingly.

"And then there's that little Vearl around here somewhere. Vearl's my former wife's boy. He don't stay at the house, here, much. It looks like he'd rather stay down at the quarters with Susan and her raft of pickaninnies."

Semon nodded some more. He wet his lips with his tongue and dried them with the back of his hand.

"That's real fine, Horey. A man nowadays ought to have a wife. I always like to visit a man who's got a wife in the house. I never stay more than a day at a place where a man hasn't got a wife."

"I sure do like to just sit here and listen to you talk," Clay said. "You talk like a real smart man. I've heard folks say that Semon Dye was the smartest man in the whole country, but I never thought I'd live to see him ride up and stop at my house.

And, come to think of it, I never ran across a man who'd ever even so much as seen Semon Dye. I've heard all kinds of tales about you, and I reckon now I'll have something to talk about, too. When they start talking about Semon Dye, I'll step right in and tell them a little something that they never heard about before."

There was a long pause. Clay was getting his breath back, and Semon was listening for sounds in the house.

"How old did you say your wife is, Horey?"

"That's funny," Clay said. "I didn't know as I'd told you her age."

"Well," Semon said, "being as how I'm going to put up here a while, I'd like to know what there is to know."

"Dene's just turned fifteen," Clay said. "She's not really grown up yet, but it don't make no difference to me because, if there's anything I like to have around me, it's a little girl like Dene just catching on how to treat a man the best way. You might say they all catch on, sooner or later, and you'd be wrong. It's not the same thing in the long run, because it's in the catching on that pleases a man like me. And I reckon a heap of them never catch on, all the way. Dene knows how to always stay just one jump ahead of me. She somehow knows just what I want her to do for me even before I know it myself. Now, that's what I'd be prone to call a real fine kind of wife."

"That's your wife?"

"That's Dene," Clay said proudly, tossing his head.

"I'll bet a pretty you don't give her a minute's rest, coz," Semon said.

Semon leaned towards Clay and jabbed him in the ribs with his stiff thumb. Clay jumped clear of the chair, yelling as if he had been shot.

"Good God Almighty, man!" he cried. "Don't never do that again! I just can't stand to be goosed!"

Semon turned away as if nothing had occurred.

"I know what you mean, Horey," he said solemnly. "I know exactly what you mean. It's anticipating. That's the word! When a girl or woman knows how to anticipate what a man is going to crave the next minute, whether it's hugging or kissing, or eating or warming, or just good old-fashioned poontang, then that's the kind of girl a man will get right out and scrap like a pack of bob-cats for."

"That's my wife?" Clay asked, leaning forward. "That's Dene?"

"That's her," Semon said, nodding and scratching his leg. "Coz, that's her all right, all right."

Clay got up and walked to the steps and back. He stood looking at Semon Dye, his eyes popping.

"I'll be doggone," he said, looking at Semon in amazement. "I'll just be doggone, if I won't!"

"What's the matter with you, Horey?"

"You talk real smart, Semon," Clay said. "I'll be doggone if you don't talk just exactly like I feel to myself."

Chapter II

SEMON leaned forward and thrust a big red hand at Clay that looked like the cured ham of a suckling pig. Clay looked at it and then, not knowing what else to do, he grasped the stiff thumb and shook it from side to side. When he had finished, he tried to turn it loose, but Semon had clasped his fingers around Clay's hand.

"It seems to me like me and you are just about the same two kind of men," he said. "Me and you ought to hit it off together in fine style after this. Let's shake hands on it, Horey."

Semon shook his hand until Clay could feel very little life left in his arm.

"I don't seem to catch on to what you're driving at," Clay said in a daze, drawing in his hand and rubbing the fingers back to life.

"It takes a girl like what-you-call-her to make a couple of men like us understand one another," Semon said. "That's us, coz. When you told me your wife was the anticipating kind, then I just naturally knew that me and you were going to get along together like two peas in a pod."

"Have you got a wife like her, too?" Clay asked.

"Me?" Semon said. "Well, no. I aint. I lost the last one I had, coz. She went to live in Atlanta three years ago."

Clay studied the tops of his brogans for several moments. He could not look at Semon then.

"I feel downright sorry for you, Semon," he said finally. "I sure enough do. But I don't know what to say about it. It looks like you was kind of figuring on me helping you out, or something. Now, me and Dene, doggone it——"

Semon stretched out his long arm and slapped Clay on the back.

"I came here to preach, Horey," he said. "The Lord God of us all sent me into Georgia to preach the wickedness out of you people. He said the worst people in the whole world live in Georgia, and I told him I'd do my damnedest with you all."

"Where did you figure on doing all this preaching?"

"In your church," Semon said. "I take it you people have got a church."

"What church?"

"The church you people have here. The Rocky Comfort church. You've got a church, haven't you?"

Clay looked across the road towards the pines.

"You sure have got me up a tree," he said at last. "If there is such a thing in Rocky Comfort, I sure don't know which way to turn to find it."

"Where do the people go to hear preaching, then?"

"Nobody hears it, not that I know about. There used to be a church up the road there, about a mile or more, at the bend of the creek, but it's been made over into a guano shed. Tom Rhodes, up there, keeps his fertilizer in it in the spring. Then, when fall comes, he puts his cottonseed in it. Tom tore out all the pews and the pulpit and split them up for stovewood. That Tom Rhodes might be the one to see about it, but it wouldn't do no good, because Tom wouldn't let you use it, anyway."

"I reckon we'll have to make use of the schoolhouse, then," Semon said after several minutes' silence. "How far away is the schoolhouse?"

"About a mile and a half. It's up there on the other side of Tom's place."

"He didn't make use of that too, did he?"

"Tom didn't molest the schoolhouse. They keep school up there three or four months of the year, some years. Tom let that alone."

"Then I'll preach in it Sunday. You can spread the word about so the people will know I'm going to preach."

"Won't be no sense in doing that," Clay said. "Everybody'll know about it, all right. Can't a doggone thing happen in Rocky Comfort without the news of it spreading like wild-fire."

Semon held up his hand.

"Shhh!" he whispered. "Who's that?"

"Where?" Clay asked. "I don't see a solitary soul nowhere."

Semon got up and walked softly around Clay's chair towards the door. When he appeared to be on the verge of running inside, Clay jumped up and beat him to it.

"Now, hold on here, Semon. What you fixing to do?"

"I heard somebody right inside one of these windows," Semon said. "I wanted to see who it was."

"Doggone it, this here is my house," Clay said. "I'll do the looking if there's any to be done."

"Go see who you can find, Horey, and bring them out here," Semon told him. "I'll sit right down and wait."

Clay looked into the hall, waiting for Semon to sit down in the chair. When Semon had seated himself, Clay tip-toed inside.

In a few minutes the sounds of somebody scuffling reached the porch. Semon got up and waited. He was at the door when Clay came through the hall, pulling Dene behind him.

"Now, she's shy of strangers," Clay apologized. "Don't be taken back if she acts scared and tries to run off. She's just turned fifteen, like I said, and she aint got accustomed to seeing strange folks yet."

Semon caught her other arm and helped Clay bring her out on the porch. When they were outside, Semon smiled at Dene and patted her lightly on the buttocks. Clay swallowed hard.

"Now wait a minute, here," he said.

"Don't get all wrought up, coz," Semon said. "I'm just trying to pacify her. It's just like stroking the wildness out of a colt. You can't do a thing with them until you stroke them some and make them forget their excitement. You being a farmer, you ought to know that."

Clay stepped forward and gave Semon a shove. Semon did not budge an inch.

"Doggone it, now," Clay said. "I don't like that one bit."

Semon smiled down at Dene, and she looked up at him. He stroked her some more.

"See there, coz?" Semon said, looking at Clay. "What did I tell you? That's all it takes to tame the wildest colt or the most fidgety woman. Seeing is believing, aint it, coz?"

Clay pushed Dene towards a chair. She sat down quickly, looking first at one and then the other. Clay felt relieved when she sat down. He glared across at Semon.

"Dene never got accustomed to a stranger like that before," he said, "but I don't reckon it was her fault this time."

"Now, just sit down and calm yourself, Horey. We're all of a color here, and there's no sense in flying off the handle. We don't want to have a falling out so soon. Especially, when I'm tickled to death to be here. I feel sort of proud to be visiting a man with such a fine-looking wife."

Dene got up from her chair and tried to leave the porch. Clay grabbed her.

"Where you going now, Dene?" he said.

"To see about supper," she told him.

"I reckon it is getting on close to the time to eat, at that. You'd better tell Sugar to cook up a company dish for supper. Semon'll be mighty hungry."

Dene got up again and ran across the porch. Long after she had disappeared from sight, Semon continued to look after her.

"Who's Sugar?" he said suddenly.

"Sugar?" Clay said. "Why, Sugar's the cook."

"Does she happen to be a colored girl, coz?"

"Sugar's that, all right, only she's not black. She's sort of yellow."

"High yellow, eh, Horey? Well, well, well!"

Semon studied the outline of the magnolia tree in front of the house, breathing deeply of the odor of the tree.

"You've got a right nice little wife, too, Horey," he said finally, nodding at Clay. "You ought to be pretty well fixed, all in all."

"Dene's all a man could beg for, I reckon. I've been married three or four or five times so far, and Dene's my pick of the lot. The one I had just before I married her was fair-to-middling. That was Lorene, whose little boy Vearl is down the road there now. Lorene was one of the finest wives I ever had, but she got so she didn't seem to give a whoop whether she pleased me or not. Sometimes I'd say she didn't care whether she stayed a jump behind all the time, or a jump ahead. I couldn't complain about Dene, though. She's always that all-fired jump ahead of me."

"You mean to say she anticipates you," Semon said. "She has that rare gift of anticipating. I see that myself now, after I've met her. You are dead right about it. She does give a fellow the notion that she's the anticipating kind."

Clay sat up erect.

"What in the doggone hell do you know about what Dene does?" he said angrily.

"I was just helping you out with the big word, coz," Semon said.

"Well, now," Clay said, "I don't give a doggone if you are a preacher, but I don't aim to have you butting in all the time like that."

"Take care, Horey," Semon said severely. "I'm a man of God, I am!"

"I don't give a hoot who you are. You aint past looking at a woman, are you?"

"Now, wait a minute, Horey. You're taking the hurdles before you get to them. Just what are you driving at, anyway?"

Clay jumped up, his fists doubling.

"I don't like for no man, be he preacher, or be he sinner, to be coming around and patting Dene on the behind like you did."

"I don't see how you can talk like that," Semon said. "I was taming her just as much for you as I was for myself, coz."

"That's all I want to know," Clay said, turning and walking heavily into the house.

Chapter III

WHEN supper was over, they walked out into the yard. The sun had set, but the hour's twilight had just begun. There was a thin layer of blue smoke hovering close to the earth. The wild-fires on the ridge that had been smoldering all day in the sun began to blaze in jagged outline against the sky.

Semon strode around the yard, looking, listening, and breathing deeply. Clay tried to keep up with him, but Semon did not notice him. He moved about the yard as restlessly as a fox in a cage.

"What's galling you, Semon?" Clay asked him, running in front of Semon and blocking his path. "I'll be doggone if I ever saw a man carry on like you do. What's tormenting you, anyway?"

Semon craned his neck to look down at Clay. In the twilight his face looked like a sheet of pebble-grain leather.

"It's like this, Horey," he said, leaning closer. "My wife has been gone from me for three or four years now, and I've never married again. Women like to stay in one place, where they can have a house and grow flowers and raise children. But I can't settle down. And as long as I'm a traveling preacher, I reckon I'll be wifeless."

"That's a doggone shame," Clay said.

He did not look at Semon. If he had had a little more nerve, he told himself, he would have advised Semon to pack up his belongings and go somewhere else before night set in. Before he could get really good and mad, Semon slapped him on the back and winked at him with one of the slits in his leather-tight face.

"I feel horny tonight," Semon said, nodding his head. "How about showing me a little fun, coz?"

He jabbed at Clay with his stiff thumb, but Clay was too quick for him. He stood back and looked up at the leather-colored face jutting into the sky.

"You know what I mean, coz," Semon said, nodding his head.

Clay caught himself nodding his own head. To save his life he could not keep from doing that.

Before he knew it, he was following Semon across the yard and running beside him in the road.

"Which house does Sugar live in?" Semon said, striding ahead no matter how fast Clay walked to keep abreast.

"Now, you don't mean Sugar, doggone it," Clay said.

He saw there was no way to stop Semon from going to Sugar's house. He hoped Hardy was not there. Just before reaching the cabin, Clay stopped.

"Don't be lagging behind, Horey," Semon said, grasping his shirt and pulling him along. "I want you to knock on the door and call her outside."

After passing the first cabin, where Susan and George lived, and where Vearl slept and played, they stopped in the road in front of the next house. There was no light in the front room, but from the kitchen they could hear sounds of laughter.

"Go on, Horey," Semon said, pushing him.

Clay found himself stumbling across the ditch into the yard. He went slowly to the back door.

Sugar was sitting in a chair at the door. She was as surprised to see Clay as he was to be there.

"Why, howdy, Mr. Clay," she said, getting up.

"You better come around to the front a minute, Sugar," he said.

She followed him around the house to the middle of the road. Semon was standing in the same tracks Clay had left him in.

"Here she is," he said. "Here's Sugar."

Semon grabbed her in the darkness before she knew what had happened. She tried to twist out of his grip, but Semon held her firmly.

"Look out there, white-folks," Sugar said. "What you trying to do to me?"

Semon put one of his arms around her and began patting her buttocks. Clay watched them with his mouth hanging open. Sugar stopped twisting and struggling and appeared to be standing still of her own accord. Clay stepped closer and watched Semon stroke her into submission.

"I'll be doggone if I ever saw the likes in all my life," Clay said. "That's the doggonest little trick I ever laid eyes on."

Semon craned his neck and looked around at Clay. There

was an opening and closing of one of his eyes that made Clay blink in admiration. He could not stay angry with a fellow who acted like that.

"There's nothing like knowing how, coz," Semon said.

Clay walked in a circle around them trying to see all that was taking place. When he got back, Semon was still patting Sugar.

"My Hardy would choke the life out of me if he caught me messing around," Sugar said.

"This is different, Sugar," Semon said. "You're not messing around with one of your own race. I'm a white man."

"And what else?" Sugar asked.

"I'm a preacher, too."

"Uh-huh! I thought so!"

Semon stroked her some more.

"Man, you oughtn't be messing around like this. Looks like you'd leave colored girls alone and attend to your business."

Clay began pulling at Semon's sleeve. He finally got him started back up the road, after Semon had told Sugar something that he could not hear.

When they were half way up the road, Semon asked him why he had pulled him away like that.

"I heard Hardy coming somewhere," Clay said. "I'll be dog-gone if I want to get mixed up in anything that you started."

They walked the rest of the way without talking again. When they got to the house, Clay started up the steps to the porch, but Semon stopped and looked back at the quarter where the cabins were. Clay went back down the steps.

"Come on in on the porch and sit down," Clay said. "I wouldn't stand up out here."

"I'm waiting for Sugar," Semon said. "She'll be along in a little while."

Clay gazed up into the leather-hard face.

"I didn't know you told her to come up here to the house. What makes you think she's coming?"

"I told her, all right," Semon said. "She'll come."

Clay sat down on the bottom step, looking at Semon all the time. He did not know what to think about a man like that.

Presently he turned around and caught Dene standing behind him looking at Semon. She did not know Clay had seen her.

"What you doing, Dene?" he said, turning around and catching her before she could get away.

"Just looking," she said.

"Looking at what?"

"At him," she said, pointing at Semon in the yard. "He's the handsomest thing."

"If I ever catch you making up to him, I'll thrash the hide off you, Dene. That's one thing I won't stand for at all."

He turned her loose, but she did not run away. After looking at Semon a while longer she sat down in the rockingchair by the door. Clay could hear her rocking back and forth, but he did not look back at her again. He was busy wondering if there was going to be any trouble that night. He knew he could not handle Semon.

Semon had gone to the road several times, only to come back

and stride up and down the yard. He did not look in Clay's direction.

Clay heard Dene stop rocking.

"He's the potentest thing," she said.

"Now, look here, doggone it all," Clay said, jumping up and running up the steps.

He ran to her chair and shook her.

Just when he was getting ready to scold her for talking the way she did, he heard Semon run across the yard to the road. Clay was able to see Sugar coming up the road.

Leaving Dene, he ran down the steps. By the time he reached the road, Sugar and Semon were coming into the yard. He walked along beside them until they reached the house.

"Now, let's stop right here," Clay said, getting in front of Semon. "This is just about far aplenty."

Semon laid a hand on Clay's shoulder and looked down into his face.

"You wouldn't stand in the way of a fellow's good times, would you, coz?"

"That all depends," Clay said. "But too far is far enough."

Sugar started backing away, but Semon grabbed her. She could not struggle much in a grip like Semon's.

"White-folks, I don't want to mess around none. You sure did get all mixed up about me."

"Now, now," Semon said, "don't start talking like that, Sugar. Just keep quiet and I'll straighten things out."

Sugar showed no signs of obeying him.

"You're a preacher, aint you, Mr. Semon?" she asked.

"I am," he said.

"Then you oughtn't be out worrying colored girls like this. If you'll just turn me loose, I'll be much obliged."

"Don't try to put me off, Sugar."

"Now, I was thinking," Clay said, stepping in, "if we would only——"

Semon reached an arm around Sugar and began patting her. She looked from Clay to Semon.

Clay had to stop talking and watch what was taking place. He had never seen anything to equal it before in all his life. Up on the porch Dene got up out of her chair, and she came as far as the top step to watch.

"Mr. Semon, you're the most devilish white man I ever saw in all my life," Sugar said.

Semon winked at Clay in the half-light, drawing shut one of the slits in his face and opening it again. He patted Sugar's buttocks while Clay watched speechless. Before Clay realized it, Semon was drawing Sugar closer to the house. They were at the steps before he caught up with them.

"Now, let's just hold on here a minute," Clay began. "If I know the first thing about anything, I know——"

Semon and Sugar mounted the steps and crossed the porch to the door. Clay leaped up the steps behind them.

When he got to the door, he could do nothing. Semon and Sugar had gone inside; he was left standing in the doorway with Dene.

He turned and looked at Dene, staring at her when she continued to look inside. He gave her a shove.

"He's the strangest man," she said.

He shoved her again, pushing her back on the porch, and went inside to find out where Semon was going.

Chapter IV

INSIDE the dark house Clay managed to find a lamp. He lit it hurriedly and ran to Semon's room. He got there before Semon had a chance to shut the door.

"Now, I'm as open-minded as the next one to come along," Clay began, "but when it comes to bringing darky girls——"

"Set the lamp on the table, Horey," Semon ordered. He waited for Clay to obey.

"When you drove up here today," Clay said, "I was mighty glad to welcome you, but——"

Semon took out his revolver and laid it on the table by the lamp. It was the first time Clay had seen it, and he was too surprised to learn that Semon carried a gun to say anything more.

The pistol was a six-shooter with a spring trigger. It was a dangerous-looking gun to find on a man like Semon Dye. Clay blinked at it in the lamplight.

"You don't have to stay, Horey," Semon said, motioning him towards the door. "You can get out."

"Well, now," Clay said, "I don't want you to think I aint as hospitable as the next one, but——"

"Coz," Semon said, "I hate to disappoint you, but it aint in my nature to play second-fiddle. You'll just have to go outside and wait."

He went to Sugar and began stroking her.

There was nothing Clay could do after that, and he backed from the room into the hall. He stood there looking inside until Semon slammed the door shut. He walked unsteadily through the hall to the porch.

Dene was standing at the door.

"He's the funniest man," she said.

Clay looked at her a moment, and then he shoved her away from the door.

"Shut up, Dene, doggone it all," he said.

When he sat down, Dene came to the chair beside him and sat down on the edge of the seat.

"I'll be doggone if I ever heard tell of a preacher like him before in all my born days," he said. "He's Semon Dye, all right, but he don't act like a preacher no more than me or Tom Rhodes."

He stopped talking and stared at the red glow in the sky over the ridge.

"He's the potentest man," Dene said, rocking a little.

"Shut up, Dene, doggone it all," he said.

There was a sound in the yard like somebody scraping shoe-leather on hard sand. Clay jumped in his seat, straining his eyes in the darkness. Dene clutched his arm, but he paid no attention to her. He moved to the edge of his seat, pulling himself forward with hands gripped on the railing.

Once he thought he caught a glimpse of a dark face in the path from the road. He was a little uneasy when he realized that the only person who might be out there was Hardy.

"Who's that?" Clay asked.

"It's me, Mr. Clay," Hardy said, coming closer to the porch.

"What do you want, Hardy?"

"I'm up here looking for Sugar, Mr. Clay. I wouldn't be bothering you if it wasn't for that."

"What makes you think she's up here?" Clay said.

"Mr. Clay," Hardy said, "please don't go trying to put me off. I know you aint that kind."

"Are you looking for Sugar?"

"Mr. Clay, you know good and well I'm looking for her. Please don't go trying to put me off, Mr. Clay."

Hardy came to the foot of the steps. From where he stood he could see through the open door into the hall. There was no light anywhere except in Semon's room.

"Did Sugar tell you she was coming up here, Hardy?" Clay asked him.

"No, sir."

"Then what makes you think she's up here?"

"Mr. Clay, don't go trying to put me off. That white man told her to come up here."

"Did Sugar tell you he said that?"

"No, sir."

Clay listened for a while. Once he thought he heard Semon, but he was not certain. There was so much going on inside his head it was hard to fix his mind on one thing and keep it there.

"What're you aiming to do, Hardy?" Clay said.

"I came up here to get Sugar," Hardy said firmly. Clay could feel the determination in his voice.

Hardy was a yellow Negro, and Clay knew he could not handle him in the same way a black Negro was handled.

"Now, Mr. Clay," he said, "there aint no use in trying to put me off no longer. I don't have no hard feelings against you, and I don't want to have none. But I came up here to get Sugar and take her home. That's what I'm standing here for now, Mr. Clay."

Clay could feel Dene moving on the edge of her chair beside him. He did not have to look at her to know that she was watching Hardy.

"I scarcely know what to say to you, Hardy," Clay began uneasily. "Semon Dye, the traveling preacher, came here to stay today, and he's got Sugar in the house, there, now. I reckon you knew that all the time, anyway."

"Yes, sir, Mr. Clay," Hardy said, coming up the steps. "I don't want to make no trouble. I aint that kind at all."

He stopped when he reached the top step.

"It's white-folks' fault," Hardy said. "I don't blame it on Sugar none. That white man got her to come up here, and she wouldn't have come if he hadn't told her to. It's the white-folks who always make trouble for the colored."

"What're you aiming to do about it, Hardy?" Clay asked uneasily.

"I came to take Sugar home."

Hardy crossed the porch to the door. Clay jumped up and beat him to the threshold.

"I wouldn't raise no rumpus in your house, Mr. Clay," Hardy told him.

"I'll go tell Sugar you came to get her," Clay said.

He left the door and walked into the dark hall without waiting to hear what Hardy said. He went to Semon's door, turned the knob easily, and stepped inside. Not until he was already inside the room did he realize that Hardy had followed him and was standing behind him.

He crossed the room and turned up the lamp.

Semon saw only Hardy. He reached for his revolver on the table beside the bed. In a leap he was on his feet and standing in front of them cocking the pistol with his stiff thumb.

"Don't point that thing at me, Mr. Semon," Hardy said angrily. "I can't stand that."

"Shut your mouth and get out of the house," Semon shouted at him. "I don't take no fooling from niggers. Get out of here, coon!"

Semon was an entirely different-looking man then. When he had arrived that afternoon, wearing his black dust-stained suit and hat, and the stringy black bow tie, he looked exactly like an itinerant minister climbing out of his car to stop and rest after a long and tiresome trip across the country. Now, in the kerosene light, against the background of yellow pitch-stained pine walls, he looked like a wild man stalking an animal in the woods.

"We'd better settle this thing peacefully," Clay said thinly, watching the gun in Semon's hand.

He was ignored. Hardy refused to back away. He came forward a few steps, watching the lamp on the table.

"Keep back, or I'll shoot you down to start with," Semon threatened. "You can't fool with me. I know how to handle yellow niggers like you."

Clay saw what was going to happen. He leaped towards the side of the room.

Hardy plunged forward, attempting to reach either the lamp on the table or the pistol in Semon's hand. He failed to get his hands on either one. When he was an arm's length away, Semon fired his revolver at him. The explosion in the chamber of the short bulldog pistol shook the frail house to its foundations. Dust fell in chunks from the cracks in the ceiling, and chips and splinters rolled from the cracks in the pine-boarded walls.

Clay was trying to make up his mind whether to try to take the pistol away from Semon, or whether to stay where he was. He stood his ground.

Hardy had fallen on his hands and knees. He remained there on all fours at Semon's feet, his head hanging downward until it almost touched the floor.

Semon was cocking the pistol again with his big stiff thumb. When the hammer was drawn back, the trigger clicked, and Semon aimed it once more at Hardy. Before he could fire it, Sugar fell across Hardy, flinging her body between them.

Semon was undecided for a minute.

"Get up and get out of here, both of you!" he said at last. "If I have to shoot again, it'll be through both of you at the same time."

Sugar was trying to lift Hardy. She soon saw she would not be able to carry him out, so she managed to drag him to the door. Semon watched them until they were in the darkness of the hall. They left the house by the back door, and not another sound was heard from them after that.

Clay knew he would not see Hardy again until either his wound had healed or his dead body was found. He and Sugar would go to the woods and not come back until that time.

It was all over then. Semon sat down in a chair, his hands shaking too much to hold the revolver any longer. He tossed it on the bed and looked down at the floor where Hardy had fallen.

There was a rank odor of burned powder in the room, mingling with the cloud of yellow dust that had been shaken from the walls and ceiling and had not had time to settle on the floor and furniture.

"I don't mind seeing a dead darky once in a while," Clay said, "but I sure do hate to see one of my hands passing away on me right at this time. It's planting time, and no other. If Hardy was to die, I'd have to get out and do some of the work myself. I sure would hate to see him pass on."

Dene had been standing outside the door in the dark, and she looked inside the room. Neither Clay nor Semon saw her, and she came inside and stood near the door with her back to the wall.

"What kind of treatment do you call this for a visitor in your house, Horey?" Semon said, turning his head to one side and glaring at Clay. "Looks like you would be on the lookout to take care of the people who come to stay with you."

Dene could not keep her eyes from going back and forth to Semon. He was a strange-looking sight to see in the lamplight, sitting hunched forward in the little chair, his underwear looking as if it had shrunk a dozen sizes since he first put it on.

"He's the queerest man," Dene said, giggling a little.

Clay looked up at her, not knowing she had come into the room. Semon did not move.

"I don't see why you think I was due to look out for you so much," Clay said. "Looks like you was the one who wouldn't ask no advice."

"He's one of those God-damn yellow niggers," Semon said. "That's the whole trouble. You ought to have told me he was that kind. I can handle the black ones, but it's dangerous to get tangled up with those yellow sons of bitches. They act like they're just as good as a white man."

Clay moved across the room, his shadow covering Dene.

"Looks to me like a man of your sense would have known Sugar's man was yellow like herself," Clay said. "Yellow girls don't do much mixing with the black ones. They nearly always pick out a man with the lightest color."

Chapter V

IT was late when Clay got up the next morning. Usually he was out of bed by five. There was never much for him to do, except to see that the darkies got started to the fields on time. Some mornings he walked down the road as far as the bridge, and turned around and came back; by seven, at the latest, he was ready to sit on the front porch and put his feet on the railing.

This morning the sun was two hours high when he opened his eyes. He lay on his side wondering why he had slept so late. It was not long before he remembered what had happened in the next room.

Clay jumped out of bed, hurrying into his pants and shirt, and went to the kitchen. Sugar was not there, but Dene had breakfast ready. He sat down at the table and ate quickly.

When he had finished, he spoke to Dene for the first time that morning. She had already eaten, and she was clearing the table.

"Where's Semon Dye?" he asked her, pushing back his chair. "You haven't seen him this morning?"

Dene made a trip to the stove and back before she answered him.

"He hasn't been out here. I suppose he's still in bed asleep," she said. "He's the queerest thing."

Clay went to the front porch, passing the closed door of Semon's room without noticing it. At the threshold of the outside door he stopped. Semon's old car was still there, standing in the green shade of the magnolia tree where he had left it. While he was standing there wondering, Semon's door opened, and out he stepped, straightening his stringy black tie and flicking dust from his coat.

Clay waited for him to come to the porch.

"I didn't know where you were," Clay said. "I was looking everywhere for you. Somehow, I didn't think you'd get up and fly off into the night."

"I feel fresh as a daisy," Semon said, beaming upon Clay. "I never felt better in my life. You take an April morning and a man like me, and the combination can't be beat. We feel like a young rooster."

"That's good," Clay nodded. "I had been thinking that maybe last night sort of did you up."

Semon looked down upon Clay, laughing.

"Things like that never upset me, Horey," he explained, rubbing his hands together. "I've never let little things like that set me bottom side up. I've got accustomed to knocking about from pillar to post. For the past twenty years I've been first here, next there, and then someplace else."

"Things like shooting darkies never upset you none?"

Semon shook his head firmly.

"You're used to winging them?" Clay said.

"Yes and no," he said; "I am and I aint."

"Now look here," Clay said, squinting up at the tall man. "If I was to ask you if you was Semon Dye, would you say that, too?"

"Coz, don't let anybody tell you different. I am Semon Dye. And don't you forget it."

"I don't reckon I'll be apt to forget it," Clay said. "I've always heard there was such a creature as Semon Dye, but I never looked for him down here in Rocky Comfort."

Semon sniffed the air in the hall. He turned and looked through the house to the back porch.

"I always like to eat a little something in the morning," Semon said. "Reckon you could fix me up?"

"Doggone my hide," Clay said, "I forgot all about you eating. Here, just walk out to the kitchen and Dene will set you a plate. I've done had mine."

Semon walked down the hall, shaking the timbers of the frail house with his long heavy strides. Just as he was about to step out on the back porch, he stopped and whispered back to Clay:

"Sugar's not cooking this morning, is she?"

"No," Clay said. "I aint seen Sugar all morning. Nor Hardy, either. Dene's cooking now. I don't know when Sugar will show up again."

Semon nodded and went out on the porch and looked into the kitchen. Clay could see him standing there, sticking his head through the door. He waited until Semon had gone inside, and then he found his chair on the front porch and sat down with his feet on the railing to smoke his pipe.

Up the road he could see Vearl and three or four Negro children playing with an old automobile tire in front of the cabins. They were rolling it as if it were a hoop, and it was so large and so heavy that it took two or three of them to move it. He watched Vearl playing in the sand and dust. Vearl's clothes were a little ragged, he noticed, but they were clean enough. Susan washed them every day. The three youngest pickaninnies were naked. They did not wear clothes at all from April to September. They were about three or four years old, and coal-black. They looked, surrounding Vearl, like crows hopping around a basket of cotton.

Susan took care of Vearl. He ate at her house, he slept there, he played in the yard and in the road all day long with the other children, and his clothes were washed in the big black iron pot with all the others. There were days when neither Clay nor Dene saw him at all; when they did see him, he was usually playing in the road with the other children. Occasionally he came to the house on an errand for Susan or George, when she needed some soap, or when George wished tobacco; and if Clay happened to be at home at the time, he always tried to catch Vearl and talk to him.

Clay had not succeeded in catching Vearl for nearly a year. Vearl knew that Dene was not his mother, and he was not certain that Clay was his father. His mother had dark hair, and she had always worn a ribbon of some kind around her hair. Dene's hair was almost yellow, and Vearl had never seen it hanging down her back as his mother had worn hers most of the time.

Clay shifted his feet on the railing and contemplated Vearl. It was the first time he had taken any notice of the boy in several days.

"That boy," he said to himself.

Vearl had been left in Clay's care when Lorene went to Jacksonville. She had said she would not be able to take care of him for a while.

That was the same time she had made him promise to take Vearl to the doctor in McGuffin and have him treated until he was well. The boy had contracted syphilis when he was three or four years old, and nothing had been done for him. The disease had run on and on for the past year and a half. Clay still intended taking Vearl to town to see the doctor, but he had postponed it so long that it had become a habit. He did buy a bottle of medicine in McGuffin for Vearl one Saturday; the bottle stood on the kitchen shelf, where it had been ever since the day he brought it home. He had never been able to catch Vearl to give him the medicine.

"That boy, Vearl," he said again, watching him dart in and out of the group of Negro children.

The boy was six years old then, going on seven, and Susan had told him several times lately that Vearl ought to be treated. Susan hated to see him in such a condition, and she was afraid her own four children would catch syphilis. She had begged Clay to take Vearl to the doctor in McGuffin; she had even started out walking with him herself one day. She would have got there, but before they had gone a mile, Vearl had broken loose from her and run across the creek where she could not catch him.

Clay knew it was his duty to take Lorene's boy to the doctor, but he could not exert himself to go to the trouble of catching him and holding him in the car all the way to town. Susan did not blame him for Vearl's disease, but she did blame him for not doing something about it.

As he sat looking up the road, Clay realized that he had not kept his promise to Lorene. But he was determined to take Vearl to the doctor in McGuffin some day. He assured himself of that.

It was then that he remembered the bottle of medicine on the kitchen shelf. He started to get up to go after it, but when he thought of the effort it would require to catch Vearl and force a dose down his throat, he sat down again. He knew the chances were that he could not catch Vearl, even if he spent the whole day trying, because the boy could shin up a tree nearly as fast as a squirrel.

He decided to wait until he could slip up on Vearl some day and grab him unexpectedly.

"That boy, Vearl," he said, spitting.

Chapter VI

U P the road beyond the cabins a cloud of dust boiled high
into the air. An automobile was throbbing through the
deep sand and yellow dust. Clay knew it was Tom Rhodes even
before he could recognize the car at that distance. He stood up
to watch its approach.

For a moment it looked as if Tom were going past without
stopping, but when he was within ten feet of the gate, he locked
the wheels and steered into the shade of the magnolia tree beside
Semon's car. He hopped out and began inspecting the strange
machine from front to back. He walked around it, kicking the
tires to see how much air was in them. When he had finished
looking at the car, he grasped the rear of it and shook with all
his might. That was all he wished to know about it. He opened
the gate and came up the walk.

"How's everything, Tom?" Clay said, moving over to the
next chair.

Tom took the seat and threw his hat on the floor.

"Couldn't be better with me."

"Going to town?"

"I thought I might drive in to McGuffin for a little while. Can't buy nothing, but looking's free."

Tom turned around and glanced into the hall through the open door. After that he turned again and looked through the window behind him.

"Heard anything?" Clay asked, dropping his voice to a hoarse whisper.

"A little," Tom nodded. "One of the darkies was telling me something about it before breakfast this morning."

Clay said nothing. There was little left for him to tell Tom. The Negroes always knew as much as anyone else, and sometimes more.

"Who is this fellow, anyway?" Tom asked.

"Semon?"

"I reckon that's his name."

"It's the traveling preacher, Semon Dye. He drove up here yesterday afternoon and said he was going to stay a while. He's aiming to preach at the schoolhouse Sunday."

"I reckon I've heard enough about him," Tom said. "Now I'd like to see what he looks like."

"He's in the kitchen eating breakfast. He'll be done in a little while. He ought to have been done long ago."

"Who's out there with him? Dene?"

"I reckon so," Clay acknowledged.

"He'll take his time then."

Clay dropped his feet from the railing and listened. He could hear not a single sound from that part of the house.

"Where'd he come from?"

"He said he came from Alabama. That's all I know about him. He won't talk much about himself, except to say that his wife left him and went to Atlanta to live."

"A lot of them do that," Tom said. "Or go to Augusta or Jacksonville."

"I reckon so," Clay said.

Tom looked around again, stretching his neck to see through the hall to the back porch. A moment later he straightened up, winking at Clay. "Here he comes now."

They waited for Semon to reach the porch. When he saw Tom Rhodes, he looked at him sharply for a moment, as if he wished to be certain he had never seen him before. He went to the vacant chair at the railing.

"Howdy," Tom said.

Semon bent his head forward and looked down into Tom's face. A smile spread across his leather-tight face.

"Live around here?"

"Up the creek," Tom said. "Folks call me Tom Rhodes."

Semon settled himself comfortably in the chair and raised his feet to the railing.

"This is fine spring weather we're having," he said.

"Can't expect much better for April," Tom told him. "It never gets good and hot in Rocky Comfort till about June or July."

The sun beat down upon the house and yard without mercy. It was between nine and ten o'clock then, and the temperature in the shade of the porch was eighty-five. By mid-afternoon it would probably be ninety-five.

"Clay tells me you're a preacher," Tom said. "I reckon he knows what he's talking about."

"I am, I am," Semon confirmed.

"Well, that's a doggone shame."

"Why is it?" Semon asked, sitting up.

"I've got a little drink out there in the car, and I'd like to be sociable with it. But being as you're a preacher, I reckon I'll have to go on off and drink by myself. Some preachers don't take to it, I've heard."

Semon laughed a little, looking at Clay.

"I started out for McGuffin," Tom explained. "Just before I got ready to leave the house, my wife came to the door and said, 'Tom, you're forgetting the molasses jug.' And sure enough I was forgetting it. But I've got it with me now, and it looks like I can't be sociable with it."

"I never heard of anybody drinking molasses," Semon said.

"It aint that, preacher. I just always manage to get the two jugs mixed up."

"Corn?" Semon asked, wetting his lips.

"The best dew in Georgia," Tom said. "I made it myself up the creek."

"Maybe you did get the molasses jug instead. Maybe when your wife was reminding you to take the molasses jug to the store, you did get the mixed up, sure enough."

"Doggone!" Tom said. "Maybe you're right, preacher. I'd better go out and see right away."

He got up and ran down the steps. When he reached the gate, Semon left the porch and followed him. Clay ran after them.

Tom pulled the jug from under the back seat and shook it. There was a smile all over his face.

"You got me rattled, preacher," he said. "You sure did. You got me so balled up I didn't know my own mind. But it's just like I thought. The molasses jug is still at home."

"Corn?" Semon inquired, coming closer and smelling the stopper.

"And ripe," Tom insisted. "I made it myself, and I ought to know good dew when I see it."

"That's a man's drink all right, all right."

Tom and Clay walked to the magnolia tree and were getting ready to sit down in the shade. Semon found himself left alone.

"Being as you're a preacher," Tom said, shaking the liquor in the gallon jug, "I don't reckon you'd take a drink of Georgia dew."

Semon sat down between them, pushing their knees out of his way to make room for himself.

"He took a liking to Sugar," Clay said. "I reckon he could take a liking to corn, too."

"Doggone!" Tom said in pretended surprise. "Is that right? I never would have thought it, preacher. Maybe I could be a preacher myself, if that's what it takes."

He pulled the stopper and held it up to Semon; but Semon handed the stopper over to Clay and stuck his stiff thumb through the glass handle and threw the jug into the crook of his arm. He raised his elbow slowly and allowed the colorless liquor to gurgle down his throat. A pint was gone when he handed it over to Clay.

Clay wiped off the mouth of the jug with his hand and drank six or eight swallows. Tom took his time when it became his turn. He never liked to be pushed when it came to drinking. He set the jug on the ground between his legs and looked at it.

"Are you aiming to preach at the schoolhouse Sunday, preacher?" he said.

"Nothing else but, coz," Semon said.

"Doggone," Tom promised. "I'll sure be there to hear you. I couldn't miss that for love or money."

He lifted the jug to his mouth and swallowed a little more than either Clay or Semon had. After he had finished, he put the stopper back and drove it in with his fist.

The April sun beat down upon the magnolia leaves over their heads. The sky was blue and cloudless, and the day had started out to be another hot one. By two o'clock that afternoon the sun would be scorching.

Presently Tom took out his watch and looked at it. He studied the open face as though he were looking at something he had never seen before. He shook his head and put it back into his overalls pocket.

"I've got to be going to McGuffin," he said determinedly. "I'll never get there and back the same day if I don't get started."

"Let's have another drink before you go, coz," Semon suggested, reaching for the jug. He took out the stopper and drank heavily. Then he handed it over to Clay. "That's a man's drink all right, all right."

"You must have been around a little in your day, preacher," Tom said.

"My day is a long way from being over yet," Semon said. "But when my day is done, it's going to have been a long one."

Tom walked towards his car with the jug. He placed it under the back seat, wrapping it carefully with a burlap bag to keep it from being broken.

He got into his automobile and started the motor. He sat with the engine running, waving to Clay and Semon. They waved back at him.

"I'll be seeing you folks on my way back," Tom promised. "I'll stop by, and we'll all have another drink."

Tom once more started to leave, but he idled the engine again and leaned far over the door.

"Look out for loaded dice, preacher," he shouted. "Don't let anybody roll you."

He was gone. The car sped down the road and rounded the bend a quarter of a mile away. But long after he had passed from sight, the dust that had been blown into the air floated over the field and drifted slowly out of sight into the woods.

Both of them were feeling good when they went back to the porch. Their step was light, and their eyes shone. Dene had watched everything that had happened, and she remained in the house out of sight. She was afraid of men when they were drinking; she was even afraid of Clay.

"We ought to make Tom a deacon," Semon said. "He's a fine fellow. I like to do things for fine fellows."

"I didn't know you was going to have deacons at the school-house Sunday."

"Sure," Semon told him. "Who'd take up the collections if we didn't have deacons?"

"That's right," Clay agreed, nodding his head. "I hadn't thought about that at all."

"Have to take up the money," Semon explained. "I couldn't bear the expense of preaching unless I was paid for it."

"I can't say as I blame you for wanting pay. That's right and proper. But you don't go to expense to preach, do you? It don't cost you anything to get your bed and board, and gas for your car won't amount to so very much."

"I always like to have a little money left over. When I pass through a city like Augusta or Macon or Atlanta, I like to have enough money in my pocket to pay my way, laying over for a day or two."

"It wouldn't take so awful much for that."

"I like the best money can buy when it comes to laying over in a city."

"That don't sound so bad," Clay said. "Maybe I'd like it myself. Reckon I could be a preacher, Semon?"

Semon jabbed him in the ribs with a piercing thrust of his stiff thumb. Clay shouted, jumping high into the air.

"Good God Almighty!" he yelled. "Don't never do that again! I can't stand to be goosed like that!"

"You don't happen to be ticklish, do you, Horey?"

"That aint no name for it," Clay said, keeping beyond reach of Semon's nubbin-like thumb. "I just never could stand to be goosed."

Semon put his feet on the railing and gazed across the yard as though nothing had happened.

"You have to have religion to be a preacher, Horey," he explained. "You can't preach unless you know what you're preaching about."

"I reckon you must be right. But maybe I'll get it at the schoolhouse Sunday."

"I'll do my damnedest to give it to you. That's my job—giving people religion."

"There's one thing about being a preacher I don't know about, though," Clay said doubtfully.

"What's that?"

"I like white girls just a shade better than I do darky ones. I don't know whether I could be satisfied with one like Sugar all the time."

"That all depends," Semon said. "Every man has his own likes. You could have white ones, I reckon, if you'd rather. It don't make much difference, in the end. Colored girls are a little easier and quicker to get; other than that, I don't know that it would make much difference—except that they know how to get 'way down like a white girl don't know about."

"I reckon a fellow could sort of get used to them," Clay said. "And he could switch around every once in a while, too, if he wanted to."

"That sounds like it might be all right, but it won't work out. It never does work out."

"Why won't it work out? What's wrong with that?"

"You get so you lose your hold, jumping around from one to the other. You forget that white girls cry when it's all over and you get ready to leave. Colored girls don't."

"Well, I'll declare," Clay said. "I never would have known that. I reckon it would spoil it some."

Chapter VII

TOM RHODES was late in getting back from McGuffin. Clay and Semon had been waiting for him all afternoon. They were afraid he had drunk the rest of the corn liquor in the jug. If he had, Clay had already decided to make him go home and bring them another jugful to take the place of that which he and Semon considered rightfully theirs.

Neither of them ate much supper. As soon as they had eaten a little grits and sweet potatoes, they got up hurriedly from the table and went back on the front porch to wait for Tom. Tom had promised to stop when he came back; they wished to be there to remind him of it when he did drive up.

Half an hour before dark Semon heard an automobile coming up the road in a hurry. Clay ran out to see if it was Tom coming back from McGuffin. In the failing light it was not easy to recognize Tom's car a quarter of a mile away, and Clay went to the middle of the road to be in a position to wave him down. He was going to stop Tom Rhodes from going on past if he possibly could.

"It's Tom, all right," he called to Semon at the gate a moment later. "I know his noise."

Semon ran out to the road and waited beside him.

Tom bore down upon them without slackening speed. Just when it looked as if he had no intention of stopping, and that he was going to run over them, he swung the front wheels to the side of the road with a mighty wrench of both arms, and the car narrowly missed them both. He stopped it and shut off the engine.

"Who's that with you, Tom?" Clay yelled at him, running to the car.

Tom leaped out on the ground as though he were a ten-year-old boy.

"You've seen her enough times to remember," Tom said. "Now, look and see if you don't."

Lorene stepped out and ran around to the other side.

"Well, I'll be doggone if I won't!" Clay said. "Where did you come from, Lorene?"

Lorene threw both arms around his neck and kissed him. She would not turn him loose.

"Where's my little boy?" she asked.

"Who? Vearl? Oh, Vearl's somewhere down there. I reckon he's played so hard today he went to sleep in Susan's house. I wouldn't bother him now. Just let the little fellow sleep till morning, and I'll go down and bring him up."

"Is he all right, Clay? Did you get him well?"

"Who? Vearl? Well, I reckon he's all right. If he's not, I'll take him to see the doctor in town the first thing tomorrow morning. I wouldn't worry about him none now."

Lorene released Clay and started towards the cabins. She went as far as the middle of the road and stopped. Clay went to bring her back.

"It won't do no good to take on about him like that," he said. "The little fellow's all right. I'll bring him up for you to see the first thing in the morning."

He had barely finished speaking when he thought he detected a familiar odor about Lorene. He bent closer, lowering his nostrils to the collar of her dress. After that he straightened up.

"Looks like you and Tom have been at that jug of his," he said accusingly. "Now, Tom promised me and Semon the rest of it. It wasn't fair for you to take it."

She laughed at him and threw her arms around his neck again. He could not protest any more after that.

"I was just dying for a drink," she said. "Tom said it was all right."

"You dying for a drink?"

"Sure."

"I didn't know you'd taken to drinking the dew, Lorene. You didn't use to do it. When did you start that?"

"Oh, some time ago. I got so I liked it."

"I reckon you did. Most everybody likes it, but I didn't know you would. You didn't use to take it."

"I've been drinking Georgia corn for the past year or more, Clay."

"In Jacksonville?"

"Yes, in Jacksonville. Why?"

"I didn't know they'd have it down that far."

Tom came between them, pulling Semon with him. Clay stepped back and went to the car to look at the jug.

"This is the preacher I've been telling you about, Lorene," he said. "I didn't lie about it, now, did I?"

"Are you a preacher?" she asked, looking up at Semon's great height.

"I am, I am," Semon replied sternly.

"He sounds like it," Lorene said, turning to Tom. "Let's go in the house so I can see him better in the light."

Clay ran between them and the gate.

"Now, doggone it all, Dene's in there," he said.

No one paid any attention to him. They pushed past him and went up the path to the house. He ran to stop them, but each time he tried to block the path either Semon or Tom pushed him aside.

"Now, wait a minute, you folks," he cried at them, standing on the steps and thrusting his arms at them. "Dene's in there, now, and you folks wait a minute."

Lorene and Tom laughed at him. Semon acted as if he had taken sides with them and was intending to follow them. He hung at Lorene's side.

"Wait a minute," Tom said. "Wait just a minute."

Clay thought at first that Tom had sided with him, but when he saw Tom running down the path to the car, he was not certain what Tom had meant. He got the jug from the back seat and ran to the porch with it.

"There's enough to let everybody get a sniff," he said, pulling the cork.

He handed the jug first to Lorene. She took a drink, making a face at the jug when she finished. Tom handed it next to Semon, and Clay had to jerk it away from him because he was afraid Semon was going to take it all. There was only one swallow left when it got back to Tom. He finished it and threw the jug on the ground.

Lorene ran into the house ahead of them. The others were only a few steps behind her. The lamp on the table in Dene and Clay's room was lit, and Dene was standing beside it. She had heard the commotion in the yard when they had first arrived, and she had been watching them from the front window.

"It's been a long time since I saw you last, Dene," Lorene said. "You've grown up since then."

"I didn't know you were coming back," Dene said, looking at Clay. "I thought you——"

"It's just a visit, Dene," Tom said, breaking in. "She just came back for a few days to see the folks."

"Vearl's down at Susan's," Dene said, moving towards the door. "I'll go get him. He's the wildest thing."

Clay stopped her, pushing her back into the room.

"Let the little fellow sleep, Dene," he said. "There'll be plenty of time for Lorene to see him tomorrow."

"I'd like to see him now," Lorene said. "It's been a year or more since I saw him. Has he grown much since I left?"

"A little," Clay said. "I'll bring him up the first thing in the morning. Just sit down and rest some now."

The others had all found chairs by that time. Everyone sat down except Dene; she still stood by the table.

"Sit down, Dene," Clay said, stretching out his feet and locking his hands behind his neck. "We're all of a color here. It's hard on your feet to stand up so much at a time. Sit down."

"You've got the strangest smell," Dene said.

"Know where I found her?" Tom asked, pointing at Lorene. "Guess where I found her, Clay!"

"Where? In town?"

"Right in McGuffin. She was standing on the corner in front of the barbershop talking to some of the boys when I happened to pass by. As soon as she saw me, she asked me where she could find you. I told her out here at home, I thought; and then she asked me if she could ride out here with me. And, now, here she is. The same old Lorene, Clay! Doggone, if it aint just like old times to see her here again."

"I'm mighty glad to see you, Lorene," Clay said. "Aiming to stay a great while?"

"Oh, I don't know," she laughed, glancing at Tom. "You wouldn't mind if I did stay, would you?"

"It tickles me to have you here, Lorene. But it makes me feel sort of foolish to be sitting in the house with two of my wives. And, on top of that, it might be against the law, or something. I don't know what the law would say about it."

"Oh, it's all right," Tom assured him. "Semon, there, is a preacher. He can fix things up to suit. Can't you, preacher?"

Clay glanced anxiously at Semon across the room. He could not imagine what Semon could do about it.

"You can fix things up, can't you, preacher?" Tom insisted. "Can't you?"

"Who? Me?" Semon said, coming back to life. He had been looking at Lorene for so long that he had forgotten that there was anyone else in the room. "You mean me?"

"We don't need anything fixed up," Lorene said. "I didn't come back to make trouble. I just came back to see Vearl and find out if he is all right."

"I've got some medicine for him," Clay said. "Don't worry about Vearl. He plays so much up the road that I don't have to bother about him none."

"He's six years old now," Lorene said.

"Is he?" Clay asked. "I clear forgot."

"It sure feels like old times to see Lorene sitting here," Tom said, rubbing his hands together. "It makes me feel real good to see her back."

"I reckon you like living in Jacksonville," Clay said. "It must be fine living in a big city like that."

"Oh, it's all right. I get tired of it sometimes, though. I was working in a five-and-ten up to about three months ago. I had to stop working there. I couldn't stand it. Being up a lot late at night made me sleepy all the time."

"The stores down there don't keep open all night, do they?" Clay asked in amazement.

"Oh, you don't understand," she said. "I worked in the five-and-ten all day, and then I was up late nearly every night. It got so after a while that I stayed up to three or four o'clock every night. That's why I had to stop working in the store."

"Why didn't you go to bed early, then?"

"Oh, Clay, you don't understand. When I started working in the five-and-ten, the men would be coming in all the time and making dates with me at night. That's when I got so I couldn't stay up all night and work all day, too."

Clay shook his head. He could not understand what she was talking about. He looked at the others in the room. All of them, Dene included, looked as if they knew exactly what Lorene was talking about. Tom was grinning.

"Don't be so stupid, Clay," Lorene said, smiling at him. "I was hustling on the side."

"Hustling?" Clay repeated.

She nodded, looking at Dene beside the table.

"Well, I'll be dogged," Clay said, shaking his head. "I still don't know what you're driving at."

"Putting out for money, Clay," Tom said, nodding.

"I'll be a suck-egg mule!" Clay said, straightening up. He glanced over to see what Semon was doing. "You mean to say you've been doing that down in Jacksonville, Lorene?"

"Sure," Tom spoke up. "That's what she's been trying to tell you. I know all about it, because I've been talking to her all the way back from McGuffin."

"Well, I'll be a suck-egg mule!" he said. "I never knew it was done that way before."

"It's that way all over the country," Tom said, nodding. "There's a couple of thousand of them up in Augusta, hustling just like Lorene's been doing in Jacksonville."

"How do you know so much about it, Tom, and I don't?" he asked bewilderedly. "I never knew a thing like that before in all my life. I thought it was done sort of free everywhere just like it is in Rocky Comfort. I've seen little presents passed out, but I never saw real money change hands over a deal like that."

"Oh, I know a little," Tom said. "I've been around some. I get off to Augusta every once in a while."

Clay continued to stare at Lorene as though she were a stranger. He did not know what to think.

During the silence, Clay looked up to see Semon moving his chair across the room. He placed it beside Lorene's and sat down, leaning towards her. His voice was so low no one else could hear what he was saying to her.

"Did you hear all that, Dene?" Clay said. "What do you know about that!"

She shook her head, looking from Lorene to him and back again.

"Ask the preacher what he thinks about it," Tom urged. "Go on and ask him; don't be scared of him."

"Semon, is that one of the things you preach about?" Clay said.

"People's habits is grist for my mill, coz," he said.

Clay looked closely at him. He did not like the way he leaned over Lorene.

"I reckon you've sort of got a free rein," Clay said sharply.

"You tell other people what not to do, but you go ahead and do the same thing yourself."

Semon was too busily engaged in talking to Lorene to notice him. He ignored Clay as if he had not heard a word.

"Leave him alone," Tom said. "Let him go ahead and talk to Lorene. I'd like to see her give him something he couldn't give away."

"I haven't got a thing in the world against Semon as a preacher," Clay said. "It's true I haven't heard him preach yet, but just the same I'm willing to grant him that for what he claims to be. That's all right with me. But I don't like it worth a doggone to have him fooling around my wife like that."

"You must have forgot. Lorene's not your wife now. You're married to Dene."

"That is true, in a way. I am married to Dene, but I've never been unmarried from Lorene."

"You can't claim both of them, Clay. They've got a law against men who keep two or more at the same time."

"The law can't touch me, if Semon thinks he can fool around with Lorene. I won't stand for it. I'll go ahead and break the law with the two of them, but I aint aiming to stand by and see him fool with Lorene. And I don't believe they ever made a law to suit me, either. There's some men who need two wives, and I'm one of them. There's plenty of times when I need two of them. There aint no use making a law against it, because that don't stop me from wanting a couple."

Tom picked up his chair and moved beside Clay. He bent his head down and said something.

"She's just a whore now. Let Semon get burnt."

"I used to think a lot of Lorene, and I can't sit here and see nothing like that go on right under my roof."

"You're married to Dene, Clay. I wouldn't blame you for putting up a fight for her. But it's different with Lorene. She's been fooling with a lot of men in the past year or so. She won't think no more of Semon than she did of all those others."

"Semon ought to be content with Sugar," Clay said doggedly.

"He ought to be, but he aint. Let him go ahead, and Lorene'll burn him for a fare-you-well."

"He ought to stay content. He ought not to want more than what's furnished him."

"That's what he ought to do, I grant you. But he aint doing it. That's why I say, let him burn."

While they were talking with lowered heads, Semon had got up. He strode across the room to the window and back again. He did not appear willing to sit down again. When he left Lorene, she waited for someone else to speak to her.

When Tom looked up and saw that they were no longer talking to each other, he took Semon by the arm and led him to a corner. He spoke to him in a whisper for several minutes. After he had finished, Semon shrugged his shoulders and said nothing. He went back to his chair and sat down in front of Dene.

"How long are you aiming to stay here, Lorene?" Clay asked.

"Maybe I'd planned to stay all the time," she smiled. "I said, maybe I had."

Clay did not know what to say to that. He wished, somewhere down in himself, that she would not leave and go back to Florida right away. He hoped something would occur that would keep her from ever going back again. He had lived with her for almost five years, and he missed her. After he married Dene, he began to forget her. But now that she was back in the house, sitting there before him, he wondered if he should try to keep her there, or to allow her to leave. He knew he could not keep both Lorene and Dene; one of them would refuse to stay in the house with the other in it at the same time. He knew without thinking that such a plan would not work out. Dene had not said anything since Lorene came home with Tom, but he could see by the way she looked at Lorene that she did not wish her to stay even for the rest of the night. There was nothing that could be done about it, though; Lorene had every right in the world to come back to see Vearl whenever she wanted to.

It was getting late. The clock on the mantelpiece was not far from right, and it was eleven by it. Tom was getting up to leave for home then. His wife would not know what had happened to him. If she had known then that he had driven Lorene out to Rocky Comfort, and was in the same room with her at that moment, she would have walked down to the Horey place to take him home. Tom's wife would take no chances with Lorene Horey.

"I reckon I'll be going home now," Tom said. "It's past me and my wife's bedtime already."

"Come back soon, Tom," Clay said. "We're always glad to have you."

"I may drop down sometime tomorrow with a new jug of corn for you and the preacher and Lorene."

Semon got up to shake hands with him.

"That was a man's drink, Tom," he said. "I've got you to thank for it."

"You'll be doing that again, then," Tom said, winking at Clay. "I'll be back tomorrow with another gallon just as good. It all comes from the same run."

He went out the door and walked down the hall to the door. No one offered to go with him.

After he had left, and when they could hear him starting his car, Semon stood up and said he thought it was past his bedtime.

"Where in the world are we going to put Lorene tonight?" Clay said, thinking of it for the first time. "Now, I don't know what to do about that."

He glanced at Dene to see if she had a suggestion to offer, but he soon saw she had nothing to say.

"If we just had another extra bed, it would be no trouble at all. But we aint, and I don't know what to do. I reckon, if Dene said so, we could all three get in the one there."

He glanced at Dene to see what effect the suggestion had made on her. He did not have to look at her again to know what she thought of the idea.

"Now, I'll declare," he said, walking up and down. "It's always the poor man who has to scheme and figure. The rich man always has enough beds to take care of whoever wants to stay."

Semon came forward.

"Let her have my room, Horey, and I'll make myself a pallet on the hall floor."

He smiled a little when he said it, looking as if he really did not mind spending the night on a hard pallet.

"I reckon that's the way it'll have to be then," Clay agreed. "It's a shame to make a preacher sleep on the floor, though."

"I won't mind that," Semon said, smiling down upon Clay. "Don't let that worry you, coz."

Clay got up and carried the lamp out into the hall. He set it on the table beside the front bedroom door and went out into the back yard. When he came back into the house, there was no one there. He went into his and Dene's room and closed the door. Dene had already undressed for bed, and he could not hear the others.

"She's the nastiest thing," Dene said.

"Who? Lorene?" Clay said. "Aw, now, doggone it, Dene. She was my finest wife back in the old days."

"She's the nastiest thing," Dene said again.

Chapter VIII

LORENE was up before Clay was awake. She dressed quickly in the early dawn and went into the next room. Dene was lying awake, and when she saw Lorene beside the bed, she drew back under the covers without speaking. Lorene shook Clay until he opened his eyes.

"Get up, Clay, and go get Vearl."

"What for?" he asked sleepily.

Dene drew the covers from her head and looked at Clay's fourth wife in the gray dawn. She did not know what Lorene had come into their room for.

"Get up, Clay!"

He opened his eyes wide and looked around the room. Presently he put out his hand and felt Dene beside him. He did not turn over to look at her.

"Go get Vearl right away, Clay. Get up this minute and get him."

"Vearl? What do you want Vearl for?"

She shook him until he could not see straight.

"Oh, all right, all right," he said.

Lorene pulled the quilt and sheet from him. She knew that was the only way to make Clay get up in the morning. Clay tried to reach for them to pull back over himself, but she pulled them down to the foot of the bed. Dene slid down as far as she could go.

Clay got up and put on his shirt and pants under the tending eye of Lorene. She threw his socks and shoes to him and went to the door to wait. When he had dressed, she followed him out of the house and down the path to the road.

All the way down to Susan's neither of them had anything to say. Lorene ran a little ahead, urging Clay to walk faster. The sun was just coming up, bright red, and the color hurt Clay's eyes. He squinted until he could barely see anything ahead.

At the cabin door, Clay called Susan. The Negro woman opened it at once. She had been watching them from the window all the way down.

"Where's Vearl?" Clay said.

"Vearl's in here asleep," Susan said. "Howdy, Miss Lorene. I sure am glad to see you again, Miss Lorene."

"How are you, Susan?" Lorene said, going to the door. "Get Vearl up right away. I can't wait to see him."

"Your little boy has got to be real big, Miss Lorene," Susan told her. "He grows just like a radish, he's that quick about growing."

They all went inside. The four children of Susan's were up and crowding into a corner. They shivered in the early morning air, clinging to the quilts they held around their bare bodies. Vearl was sound asleep in Susan and George's bed.

Lorene ran and picked him up in her arms, hugging him to her breast and kissing him frantically. She could hardly believe her own eyes; he had grown a lot in a year and a half. He was getting to be a big boy now.

"Vearl! Vearl! Don't you know Mother? This is Mother, Vearl!"

He woke up and started to cry.

"I'm going to take him up to the house now, Susan," she told her.

Susan followed her to the door.

"Miss Lorene, do you aim to take him away?"

Lorene did not answer her.

"It would break my heart to see the little fellow go now," Susan said, unashamed of the tears that fell from her eyes.

Lorene ran out into the yard and started up the road with Vearl holding her tightly around the neck. She did not hear anything that Susan said.

When Clay and Lorene reached the middle of the road, Vearl was wide awake. He looked at Lorene strangely, struggling to get away from her.

"Don't you know me, Vearl?" she asked fearfully, kissing his face and arms. "Don't you remember Mother? This is Mother, Vearl! Look at me!"

"He's got pretty wild," Clay said. "In another month or two he would be as scary as a rabbit. Couldn't nobody catch him, 'less it was Susan."

Lorene held him tightly in her arms. He was heavy, and the dust in the road was deep, but she did not mind. She held Vearl as though she would never turn him loose again as long as she lived.

"This is Mother, Vearl. Don't you remember Mother?"

"We'd never have caught him if we hadn't got him while he was asleep," Clay said, walking fast in order to keep up. "He's a little wild-cat."

"Mother sure is glad to see you, Vearl. I thought I'd never get back to see you. Did you miss Mother?"

"Where've you been?" he asked her.

"Down in Florida, Vearl."

"That's where the oranges grow. I've seen them."

"Yes," she said. "Just lots and lots of them grow down there, Vearl."

"Did you bring me some?"

"I'll get you some in the store in McGuffin, Vearl," she said. "I couldn't carry any with me. They are too heavy to carry all the way here."

"Danny and Jim's poppa brought them some from Florida," Vearl said.

Lorene glanced at Clay.

"Those are some of the pickaninnies up the road a little way," he told her. He knew she would not know any of the Negroes living up there. "Pete drives an orange truck. He goes down to Florida for a load of oranges and tangerines for Ralph Stone sometimes."

They hurried the rest of the way in silence, and when they reached the gate, they saw Semon Dye standing on the front porch. He motioned to them to hurry.

"Dene's got breakfast ready and waiting," he said. Without waiting for them, he went through the hall to the kitchen.

There was a chair for Vearl, which Dene placed at the table, but Lorene insisted on holding him on her lap. He ate his grits and drank his coffee hungrily, unmindful of anyone in the room. Lorene did not begin to eat until he had finished.

"Give me some more coffee," he told Clay.

Clay went to the stove for the pot and filled his cup. Clay had finished eating, and he did not sit down again.

"Here's this bottle of medicine I got for him in McGuffin," he said, taking the dusty bottle from the shelf and setting it on the table in front of Lorene. "I've never got around to giving it to him yet."

Lorene looked at the bottle a moment and set it aside. Vearl reached for it, but she put it beyond his reach.

"You'd better take him to the doctor in town," she said.

"I've been aiming to do that," Clay said.

"Go and get ready to take him now."

"Now? Today?"

"Of course. Vearl needs a doctor right away. I can tell."

"I don't know about taking him today," Clay protested. "I hadn't thought about doing that. Wouldn't tomorrow do just as well?"

"I mean right now," Lorene told him emphatically. "Vearl needs to see the doctor before it's too late to do any good."

Clay went out on the back porch and got a drink from the bucket on the stand. He spat out a mouthful before he swallowed any. Then he went down the steps towards the barn where his car was standing under the shed. He knew there was no use in trying to argue with Lorene after she had made up her mind that something was to be done. He had never succeeded in bettering her in any argument.

The car started up without any trouble, and he backed it out and turned around in the yard. He waited for Lorene to bring Vearl out and put him in the seat beside him.

Lorene finished washing Vearl's face and hands on the back porch. She combed and parted his hair, and buttoned all the buttons on his clothes.

"I don't reckon tomorrow would do just as well, would it?" Clay said. "Tomorrow's Saturday, and I like to go to town a lots better on Saturday than any other time."

Lorene did not answer him. She placed Vearl on the seat beside Clay and closed the door. When they were ready to go, she leaned over and kissed him good-by.

"Take him to the doctor and have him treated, Clay," she instructed. "If you don't, I don't know what I won't do to you. Vearl needs to see a doctor right away."

Clay nodded glumly and drove off. He did not look back. Lorene went as far as the front gate to watch them, and when they had passed from sight down the road, she walked slowly back to the house.

Semon was waiting for her.

"I wonder where Tom is," he said. "He promised to come back today."

"I don't care where Tom Rhodes is, now or any other time," Lorene said curtly.

She sat down on the porch and looked down the road in the direction in which Clay and Vearl had gone.

Semon sat silently for a while, waiting until she was in a better mood. Presently she turned back to look at the magnolia tree at the fence.

"Tom said he was coming," Semon began again. "If he said he was, he ought to keep his word."

"He'll forget about it," she told him. "I know Tom Rhodes. You can't depend on him too much."

"You didn't know him before you left and went away, did you?"

"A little."

"He acted like he was real friendly with you yesterday. I thought you might know him pretty well."

"I used to know a lot of men in Rocky Comfort before I went to Jacksonville over a year ago. Tom was one of them." She was silent a moment. "Tom was the first one I knew."

"I've been thinking that maybe you'd like to ride back with me," Semon suggested, moving his chair closer. "Next Monday morning I'm leaving for South Georgia, and I wouldn't mind going all the way to Florida. That is, if you're going my way."

"I wouldn't like to go off with you and get into trouble," Lorene said. "How do I know about that?"

"I'd see after that part," Semon promised, pulling his chair still closer. "I'll take you to Jacksonville. I've been thinking that maybe I ought to go to Florida. The Lord's been talking to me about going down there, but I've put it off and put it off till I'm almost ashamed to think about it now. But I've made up my mind to go Monday."

"All right," Lorene said. "I'll go with you Monday."

Semon leaned forward and put his hand on the back of her chair.

"Maybe we could stop off along the way a little," he suggested.

"What for?"

"Well, just to stop and break the journey. We could stay a day or two along the way, and still get there soon enough."

"That would cost a lot, staying at a hotel."

"I figure that maybe we can make expenses without much trouble."

"How?"

"I could sort of speak of you to a few people and get them interested."

"I see," she said, nodding. "That's all right with me, just as long as everything is split fifty-fifty. But if you hold out on me, there's going to be hell to pay. I'll make it hot for you, Semon Dye, if you don't split even. I don't take chances with men like you. It's going to be businesslike."

Semon removed his hand from the chair and sat up erect, nodding in agreement.

"That's fair enough."

"Do you know how to go about it without getting into trouble? I don't want to get thirty days in some little cross-roads jail in South Georgia."

"I know my way around pretty well," Semon assured her. "I've had a little experience that way one time or another. You don't have to worry about that."

Lorene regarded him for several moments.

"Look here," she said severely, looking him straight in the eyes. "You talk like you do know your way around."

"I've had a little experience," he said. "A little."

"That's how I had you figured out."

He leaned forward once more, placing his arm over the back of her chair and lowering his head close to hers.

"I've been thinking that maybe we can get started right here before Monday. If Tom Rhodes comes down here today, we ought to be able to get a little money out of him." He waited to see what effect that had on her. "He looks like the kind of fellow who would pay his way."

"You've picked the wrong one there," Lorene laughed. "Tom wouldn't pay money. He used to throw me down for nothing when I lived here. No, Tom wouldn't start paying now."

Semon was not through.

"There's Clay," Semon intimated. "What's wrong with trying him?"

Lorene laughed at him.

"That's silly. Clay wouldn't, either. It's a crazy idea of yours to think Clay would. I used to be married to him. Why should he?"

Semon turned to contemplate the magnolia tree in front of the house. After a while he turned back to Lorene.

"I think I can work it," he stated. "If Tom Rhodes comes down here with that jug of his again, it ought to work out as slick as grease."

She turned suddenly and looked Semon straight in the eyes. A faint smile came to her lips. She knew men who planned just as he did, but none of them had worked in a guise like Semon's.

"What are you, anyway?" she demanded. "Are you a preacher or a pimp?"

Semon looked offended. He sat up and glared down at her angrily.

"I'm a man of God," he said sternly. "And don't you forget it, either."

"You get him to agree, and I'll do my part," she said at last. "But it looks to me like you're crazy. Trying it with Clay won't work. He wouldn't give you a dime."

"We'll see, we'll see," Semon said. "You do just like I tell you, and we'll see."

He got up and stood beside her chair, looking down at Lorene and contemplating her.

"I'm going to take a little walk up the road," he announced. "I might see Tom Rhodes up that way."

Chapter IX

IT was a hot and tiresome walk through the sand and dust to the house where Tom Rhodes lived. Semon had to stop several times to rest beside the road. At last he got within sight of the place, and by that time he was dusty and short of wind. He had had to take off his coat half way there, and he swung it at his side trying to fan the burning heat away.

There was no one to be seen at Tom's house when he first got there. As he went towards the barn, however, he saw a Negro man shucking corn in the door of the crib. He called the man to him.

While the colored man was shuffling towards him, Semon found shade under a willow. The heat was coming down with more intensity than ever, and he was not accustomed to walking in the hot sun.

"Where's Mr. Tom?" he asked the Negro.

"He's out around the barn somewhere. Do you want to see Mr. Tom?"

Semon nodded wearily, fanning himself with his wide-brimmed black hat.

The man went off towards the barn, stirring up the dust with his wide-soled shoes. He was gone for several minutes. When he came back into sight, he pointed his hand at Semon. Tom came around the corner of the barn a moment later.

"I was afraid you'd forget your promise," Semon said.

"What promise?"

"That you were going to bring another jug down to Horey's house."

"I'll be doggone," Tom said, coming into the shade. "Did I say that? I must have forgot all about it."

"I thought you might. That's why I walked up."

"You're hell on Georgia dew, now, aint you, preacher?" Tom laughed. His red face shook with mirth. "You're the drinkingest preacher I ever saw in all my life."

"Corn whisky is a man's drink," Semon said. "And I'm a man. I reckon that's why I like it so much."

"You just wait till I send for some," Tom told him. "It won't take long to get it."

He walked off immediately, calling the Negro. Semon sat heavily on the ground, leaning back against the willow and fanning himself in the shade.

Tom came back, urging Semon to get up.

"We'll get in the car and be ready to leave as soon as that darky gets back. It won't take him long. He's only got to go down to the cow shed in the pasture a little way."

Semon pushed himself to his feet and followed Tom to the barn, where the automobile was standing in the sun. They got in and Tom started the motor.

"Make much time with Lorene last night?" Tom asked, nudging Semon with his elbow. "It didn't use to take long to do that. Not after she made up her mind to leave, anyway. But I don't reckon she's changed much in a year or two. She still looks the same to me."

Semon understood then that Lorene knew what she was talking about when she had said that Tom would not fall into their scheme. Semon set that idea definitely aside.

Frank, the colored man, brought the jug and set it in the back of the car. He had spilled a little of the liquor on the outside when he had filled it hurriedly from the keg, and the fumes came up like flame out of the rear seat. Semon sniffed the odor greedily. He was ready to go back to the Horey place.

The car made good time through the deep sand. Tom did not bother to slow down when he came to an unusually deep bed of sand; he opened the throttle wider. Once the car leaped almost over the ditch, but Tom did not slacken his rate of speed. He kept on going, sometimes not even looking at the road ahead. Semon was relieved when they reached Clay Horey's.

"Are you aiming to preach at the schoolhouse Sunday?" Tom asked him as they stepped out of the car.

"I am, I am," Semon stated resolutely.

"What are you aiming to preach about?"

"Oh, various things," Semon said. "This, that, and the other."

"I reckon you've got such a lot of sermons all made out that all you have to do is just call them up, and they're all ready to be said."

"That's right," Semon replied shortly, watching the jug as it was lifted out of the back seat.

Tom held up the gallon jug, shaking it slightly.

"The drinks are on me, preacher. Just help yourself."

Semon pushed his finger through the glass handle and drew the jug closer.

"I'll down my share," he said; "and there's enough for others who like it, too. Everybody ought to get his fill today."

"There's more where that comes from. And more in the making. I never let myself run short this time of the year."

While they were drinking, they saw Lorene run out on the porch and look down the road. A moment later she was running down the path towards them, and they turned and saw Clay coming up the road from McGuffin.

"Here comes Clay back now," Semon said, watching Lorene.

"It didn't take him long," Tom said; "but I reckon he got tired of loafing around town on a week-day. If it was Saturday, he wouldn't have left McGuffin till midnight."

Clay turned into the yard and drove towards the barn without speaking to them. He looked as if he were in a hurry to get under the shed.

Lorene ran after him, and she got there just as Clay was walking from the car.

"Where's Vearl?" Lorene asked excitedly.

Clay walked to the house as though he had not heard her. She ran and caught up with him, pulling his arm.

"Where's Vearl, Clay?"

They had reached the porch by that time, and Tom came through the hall carrying several tumblers.

"Vearl?" Clay said, looking as if he had been taken by surprise. "Oh, Vearl got loose from me. He jumped loose from me before I got more than a mile or so away. I don't know where he is now. I reckon he went up the creek, though. He'll show up at Susan's before dark. He don't ever stay away all night."

Tom filled the glasses, placing one in Lorene's hand. Semon picked up two and gave one of them to Clay.

"And you didn't take Vearl to see the doctor?" she asked, biting her lips.

Clay drank half of his glass and set it on the floor beside him. Semon promptly filled it up again and handed it back to Clay.

"Vearl? No. I didn't get him all the way into town. But I happened to run into the doctor, though, and I said something to him about it. He said to give him the bottle of medicine, and bring him to town the next time I came in."

"I should have taken him myself," Lorene said coldly. She glared at Clay. "I might have known you wouldn't."

"I done the best I could, Lorene," he said meekly. "That's the truth, if I've ever told it, too. I wouldn't run counter to you if I could help it."

"You didn't half try," she said. "You didn't want to take him, and you didn't try to keep him in the car. You let him jump out because you didn't want to bother with him."

She drank the glass of liquor and set it down heavily on the floor beside the chair. Semon picked up Clay's glass and handed it to him. He raised his own, urging Clay to follow his lead. Clay drank and wiped his mouth.

Clay took out his harmonica and tapped it on his knee. He drew it across his mouth two or three times.

"Let's have a tune, Horey," Semon urged.

Clay blew several notes and shook his head.

"It's a little too early in the day for music," he said, shaking his head from side to side. "I can't be playing a mouth-organ before dinnertime."

After he had replaced it in his pocket, Semon urged him to drink some more.

"Where's Dene?" Clay demanded, placing the empty glass at his feet.

"She's around here somewhere," Tom told him. "I saw her in the kitchen just now when I was after the glasses."

Clay looked across at Lorene. She was sipping the brimming glass Tom had only a moment before refilled. With several glasses of corn whisky inside of him, Clay liked to look at her. She wore well-fitting clothes, and her dark hair made something turn over inside of his mind.

"Now, there's a woman for you," he said, pointing at her with one of his fingers.

"Who?" Tom said.

"Lorene, there."

"I wouldn't say too much about her, Clay. Dene is around somewhere. She'll be listening."

"That's right," Clay said. "I clear forgot about Dene. Now, Dene's a woman for you."

"How about Sugar, Clay? Is she one for you, too?"

"Aw, shucks, Tom. You know good and well I don't mess around with Sugar no more."

Semon smiled all around. He was delighted with the progress he was making with Clay. He decided to let him talk a little while longer in the hope that he could press another glass of corn upon him.

"Dene satisfy you, Horey?" Semon said, winking at Lorene and nodding approvingly.

"Dene? Well, I reckon! And then some. Why, Dene can stay a jump ahead of me all the doggone time. I never have to know my own mind around Dene. She's always giving me what I crave long before I know I crave it. And she's always been like that. When I used to see her down there in front of her daddy's house, she used to come up and give me a kiss on the sly, and a big hug—just like that! Soon as I got it, I knew I wanted it. But not till then. Dene never has got behind yet. She stays that jump ahead all the time."

"That's her way of anticipating you," Semon said.

"That's it!" Clay shouted. "That's the big word! I never can think to say it myself, but what's the use, anyhow? You're always here to tell it to me."

"I've noticed that in her myself," Semon nodded.

"What in her?"

"I've seen how she anticipates what a man wants."

"She didn't do that to you, did she?"

"I didn't say that. I said I noticed it in her."

Clay scuffed his feet over the floor as though he were going to jump up. Instead, he sat up straight and looked at each of the faces around him.

"She'd better not do it. And you'd better not do it. If I was to catch you and Dene playing that game of staying just a jump ahead, I'd—I'd——"

"You got me wrong," Semon assured him hastily. "I was merely telling you what you didn't know. You're always talking about what she does, but it takes me to fit the word in for you."

"Well, as long as that's all you do, and nothing else, it's all right by me."

Semon filled his glass, winking at Lorene. She got up and left the porch immediately.

"Where's she going?" Clay asked.

Semon shrugged his shoulders. After Clay had taken several swallows, Semon sat down on the railing in front of him and leaned forward.

"I'd like to have a little talk with you for just a minute," he said, nodding towards Tom.

They got up and crossed the porch to the other side.

"What's up?" Clay asked, lowering his voice so Tom could not overhear.

"If I was to tell you something, would you like to hear it, coz?"

"Maybe I would, and maybe I wouldn't. What's it about, anyway?"

"You're feeling good, aint you?"

"Like the world on fire," Clay stated.

Semon stooped down until his face was on a level with Clay's head. He glanced behind him to see if anyone were listening. Clay followed his lead and glanced anxiously over his shoulders.

"How'd you like to meet somebody, coz?"

"Who? Where? Who is it?" he whispered breathlessly.

Chapter X

SEMON came closer, shutting off Clay's view of Tom Rhodes at the other end of the porch.

"There's a girl out there who'd like to see you, Horey. Feel like going to see her?"

"You're doggone right! Where is she?"

"Never mind about that. I want to find out if you're anxious to see her."

"White girl?"

"Sure, she's white. I wouldn't bother you if she wasn't."

"Doggone my hide!" Clay exclaimed. "Let's go!"

They left the porch without looking in Tom's direction. When they had gone around the corner of the house, Semon stopped him abruptly, pulling his arm.

"You've got a little money, haven't you, Horey?"

"Money? Maybe a little. What do you want to know that for?"

"Well, it's like this. You ought to give her a little something for seeing her. Now, don't you think that would be fair and square?"

"How much money?"

"Three dollars would be just about right."

Clay drew back, shaking his head slowly. His face fell, and disappointment sobered him momentarily.

"I haven't got but a lone solitary dollar between me and the world. I had to buy some gas in McGuffin to get home on, and I fooled around in a little crap game for a while. A dollar's all I got left."

Semon bit his lips in annoyance.

"Are you sure, Horey? Look in your pockets and make sure. You ought to have more than a dollar. Anybody would have a dollar; you ought to have two or three, anyway."

Clay searched carefully through all his pockets, but all he could find was a single worn and soiled dollar bill. He held it up for Semon to see.

"Maybe you could borrow some from Dene," Semon said.

"Dene? Dene hasn't got a red penny to her name. She never has money except when I give her some, and there hasn't been need of that for a long time. Dene wouldn't have any, I know."

Semon walked up and down. He finally turned and looked at Clay.

"You give me the dollar then. And if you get hold of more before Monday, you can give me the rest."

"That's a lot of money to pay for just looking, aint it? I declare, it looks to me like it is."

"You can do more than that if you want to. The sky's the limit, Horey. You've paid your money, now go ahead and get your value."

Clay watched Semon fold the bill and put it into his pants, pocket. He was on the verge of backing out of the deal when he saw his dollar go into Semon's pocket. He made a desperate attempt to reach it, but his hand was slapped down.

"I thought you said I was paying her," Clay stated. "Don't look like you ought to be putting my money in your pocket."

"I'm keeping it for her," Semon said shortly.

He took Clay by the arm and led him towards the barn. After they had gone several steps, Clay pulled loose.

"Now, wait a minute. Where's this you're taking me?"

"To the barn," Semon said, reaching for his arm.

"I can't figure out what anybody would be doing in my barn. I've been living here on this place for a long time, and I never saw anybody in it before."

"A lot of things go on that you don't know nothing about, Horey. Come on."

They walked to the barn and went inside. There was no one to be seen. The stalls were open, and the harness room door was open. Semon looked around unfamiliarly for a moment, and then he saw the ladder to the loft.

"Let's go up here," he said, pushing Clay to the ladder.

"There's nothing up there but some bundles of fodder and a little pea-vine hay," Clay protested. "I know what's up there. There aint no use in climbing the ladder just to see fodder."

Semon pulled him to the ladder and pushed him up the first rung. After once starting, they went up quickly.

When they reached the loft, they both stood up. Lorene was standing against one of the center uprights.

"I'll be doggone, if I won't!" Clay exclaimed. "What are you doing up here in the loft, Lorene?"

She beckoned to him with her finger.

Clay turned to Semon to find out what it all meant. Semon nodded at him, and gave him a shove towards Lorene. He stumbled around over the bundles of fodder, kicking up a cloud of dust.

"You've paid for it, Horey; now, go ahead," Semon told him.

"Why, that's Lorene," Clay protested. "You said there was somebody out here who wanted to see me. And I went and gave you all the money I had. That's Lorene, there."

"You paid me to see Lorene," Semon asserted. "And there she is. Now, go ahead, Horey."

Clay was bewildered for a while. He looked first at Lorene and then at Semon, and then he stared at the fodder under his feet.

"Doggone," he said. "I never knew I was paying all my money to see my fourth wife. I declare, I don't seem able to figure it out. Looks like to me you folks is just playing a joke on me. I never heard tell of a man paying money to see his wife before. True, she aint my present one, but she's my fourth one, just the same."

"By God," Semon said threateningly, "you've paid me the money, and now you're going to get what's coming to you for it. You've got to take what you bought and paid for. I'm not going to have you going around here saying I cheated you out of it. Now, go ahead, Horey. I'm not going to stand for no more foolishness. I mean business, and I don't mean maybe, neither."

Semon looked around hastily for a weapon of some kind. There was a pitchfork standing under the eaves of the roof, and he jerked it up.

"Don't look like a preacher ought to be so all-fired cussed," Clay said. "You ought to leave me and Lorene alone."

Semon raised the pitchfork, advancing on Clay, and jabbed it at him three or four times. Clay moved away from the sharp prongs and got beside Lorene.

Lorene had sat down on a bundle of fodder, and Clay saw her at his feet when he looked down. She waited, without a word, looking up at him. She did not smile, and there was a grim line at the corners of her mouth.

"You don't act like you used to, sometimes," he said, looking down at her.

"I can't afford to be easy," Lorene said. "If I did that, I'd get cheated out of nearly all that was coming to me."

"Being as it's me," Clay said, "it looks like you ought to break down and smile just a little instead of looking so hard at me. I declare, you almost scare me out of my skin—you and Semon put together."

"Now you folks stop talking so much," Semon said, prodding the air between them with the pitchfork. "The first thing I know, both of you will be scrapping me to get the dollar back. I won't stand for that. I've earned my share of it. Now, go on and stop your foolishness."

"You'd better give me my share now," Lorene said, holding out her hand. "As long as this's business, I don't want any misunderstanding later. Just give it to me now, Semon Dye."

"I haven't got change for it now, Lorene. As soon as I can get it, I'll give you yours. If I can't get it before then, I'll make change out of the collection Sunday."

"Are you still aiming to preach at the schoolhouse?" Clay asked, watching the pitchfork.

"I am, I am," Semon said. "That's what I came here for. I'm going to preach nearly all day Sunday."

"Looks like you sort of got side-tracked, then. First you say you're going to preach, and now you're out bargaining about money to see Lorene. It don't look to me like the two go hand-in-hand. Maybe they do, but it don't look like they ought to, somehow."

"Stop arguing, Clay, and get down here," Lorene said, pulling at his hand. "So much talking back at each other won't do any good."

She pulled Clay down on his knees beside her. Clay waited for Semon to go down the ladder; but he sat down on a bundle of fodder instead, showing that he had no intention of leaving the loft.

"I don't reckon anybody else will be prowling around out here and come up the ladder," Clay said uneasily. "There's Tom here. He might take it into his head to look around."

Lorene ignored his concern. She pulled him closer.

Semon was observing them coldly. He did not turn around to look the other way, and he acted as though he were an invited guest.

The moment when Clay felt Lorene's arms around his neck he forgot that anyone else was there. He kissed her to the quick.

"This feels like old times, don't it, Lorene?" he said huskily.

Her arms were tight around his neck, but she squeezed him more tightly. He had to fight for breath.

When he saw the flaring curves of her hips and the lissom swell of her breasts, he forgot all that had gone before. She no longer had to hold him with her embrace. Clay fell upon her, gouging his fists into her breasts and searching eagerly for her lips. Lorene had always been like that to him, but he had not realized until that moment how much he had missed her.

Semon had been forgotten. He had been apart from them, and it was hard for Clay to remind himself of him. He heard Semon speaking, his voice carrying as if from a great distance, but he did not try to hear what was being said. He was not interested, anyway.

Lorene was smiling at him and running her fingers through his hair. He closed his eyes and seeped himself in his thoughts of her.

Presently Clay turned his head to one side, his face pressed warmly against Lorene. His eyes were open, but nothing did he see.

"I don't reckon there's ever been anybody like us," he said for her to hear,

She tried, until tears came to her eyes, to hold securely their ultimate possession.

"It used to be like this all the time, didn't it, Clay?"

He nodded, looking at her.

Semon was standing over them then. He looked down upon them, urging them to leave the loft.

"I'll be back again sometime, Clay," she promised. "I won't stay away always. I'll come back."

He nodded again, accepting her word.

Semon had tossed the pitchfork aside, and he was waiting impatiently. He walked back and forth beside them, trying to separate them from their thoughts.

"It'll be all right if you're satisfied with Dene until I come back the next time. I can satisfy you better, but I can't stay. It's too late now. I've got to go back to Jacksonville where I belong. Maybe when I get tired of staying there, and if you stop liking Dene, I'll come back to stay some day. I'd rather do that than anything else, after I'm through with Jacksonville."

On the way back to the house, Lorene and Clay walked side by side, and yet several feet apart. Semon followed several paces in the rear. None of them had anything to say on the way to the porch. They walked slowly, not seeming to care how long it took them to get there.

Dene and Tom Rhodes were there. Tom winked, smiling at all three of them. He had known what would happen when they left for the barn.

"Dene's been asking me where you folks went to," he said. "I didn't hardly know what to answer her."

No one said anything; yet all eyes were directed at Dene. Clay did not wish to look at her then, but he could not help himself.

After they had seated themselves, Dene looked boldly at Clay.

"Where've you been, Clay?"

Clay looked off into the woods along the creek on the other side of the road. He looked at the tops of the trees, at the blue sky overhead, and at the row of sagging fence posts that bordered the road.

"Where did you go just a while ago, Clay?" she asked persistently.

"Who? Me?"

He glanced at Dene to see her nod her head.

"When? Just now?"

He looked again to see her move her head slowly up and down while her eyes bored into him.

"Where? Oh, just out around the barn," he said.

He did not look at her after that.

"Dene said she couldn't figure out what you folks were doing out there all that time," Tom said. "I told her that maybe you and Semon and Lorene were digging fishing worms."

Clay hoped the questioning would stop there. When Dene said nothing more for a while, he thought it had stopped. But later, after thinking about it, he realized that the questioning had just begun. Dene would keep him awake night after night asking him, begging him, threatening him; and she would not stop until he had told her where he had been and what he had done there. But even that would not be the end; Dene would worry him for months afterward, making him talk about it. Clay did not know what he could do about it, though. He would just have to let her talk.

"I don't reckon there's an organ in the schoolhouse," Semon said, not to anyone in particular. "We can get along without it

Sunday though, I reckon. Somebody ought to bring a fiddle or a banjo, and we can raise a tune with that. I never have much trouble with the music and singing at a meeting. People like to sing in a church or schoolhouse when they all get together. Looks like sometimes they'd a heap rather sing than listen to the sermon. I've figured it out so as to give half the time to one, and half to the other. That pleases almost everybody."

Clay took out his harmonica and tapped it on his knee. After that he ran his fingers over it to wipe off the tobacco dust from his pocket. When he was satisfied with it, he began playing.

"What are you aiming to preach about Sunday, preacher?" Tom asked. "You didn't exactly ever say, did you?"

"Preach about? About sins. I always preach about sins, Tom. There's nothing else the people will put up with, for any length of time. And the more sins, and the worse sins, and the reddest sins, I can preach about, the better the people like to listen. I believe in preaching about the things the people want to hear. I've found out what the people want to hear, and I give it to them."

"How can you tell what folks like to hear?"

"I tell by the size of the offering they drop in the hat, and by the number that come through with religion. I've been preaching long enough to know just what people everywhere want to hear."

"I reckon you know all about it then," Tom said.

"Know all about it? Sure, I know all about it." He stopped until Tom had filled his glass from the jug. After swallowing half of it, he continued. "I know just about all there is to know.

I've been traveling over Georgia and Alabama since I was twenty years old, and I'm nearly fifty now. That's why I know so much about preaching. If I had sat down in one church, like most of the preachers do, and not got out among the people, I wouldn't know a bit more than the settled preachers know. But I travel. I'm a traveling preacher, and I know just about every sin there is in Georgia. And then some!"

Chapter XI

LATER in the afternoon, after Lorene and Dene had gone into the house to take a nap, Semon left the porch without comment and walked around the corner of the building. Tom and Clay followed a minute later to see what he was doing around there.

Semon was sitting on his haunches near the brick chimney, rolling a pair of dice on the hard ground. He did not look up when they approached.

"That's my game," Tom said enthusiastically. "How'd you know it, preacher?"

Semon went on rolling the dice, snapping his fingers occasionally, and did not bother to look up. The easy rhythm of his motion made it plain that he had had much practice.

Tom sat down in front of him, squatting on his heels, and watched the cubes tumble over the hard white sand.

"Let's have a friendly little game," Tom suggested, unable to hold himself back any longer. "I don't know a better way to pass the time of day."

Clay also had become magnetized by the dice. He rubbed his fingers together, hoping to get a chance to touch them.

"It's going to be a friendly game," Tom insisted. "I wouldn't like to have it end up in a scrap."

Semon nodded assent. He looked over at Clay.

"How about it, Horey?"

"Doggone right!" Clay said, shifting the weight of his body to his other heel and scooping up a handful of sand to sift between his fingers.

"Got any money?" Semon inquired casually, rolling the dice and watching them come to a stop with a spinning motion that loosened the sand.

"Sure, I've got money," Tom said. "Least, I've got enough for a friendly game."

He pushed his hand into his overalls pocket and brought out the money he had.

"How're you fixed for money, Horey?" Semon asked, still intent upon the movement of the dice after they left his hand.

"Well, I don't know," Clay said. "The fact is, I aint got a red penny to my name. That dollar was everything I had. Maybe if you could lend it to me, I might could make it up and pay you back."

Semon shook his head decisively.

"Now, that's just too bad," Tom said. "I'm just itching to get in a friendly little game."

"If you won't lend me the dollar, I don't know how to get in the game," Clay said, watching the dice.

"That's the surest way in the world to make enemies,

Horey," Semon said determinedly. "I've never known it to fail. Lending money to start a crap game always ends up in trouble. You'd better stay out if you can't pay your own way. Man to man, now, I'd lend you the money; but a game of craps is something else. People get killed over little things like that."

Clay looked sick. He wished so much to have a hand in the game that he did not know how he was going to stand being kept out.

"Now, that's real bad," Tom said sympathetically. "I hate to see a man have to stay out of a game just because he don't happen to have a little change on him at the time."

Semon shook his head with determination.

"It's put up or shut up," he stated. "This is like anything else that's real. Most people think they can shoot crap and not have to pay. That's why I said anybody in this game would have to put up his own money—and on the barrelhead. When it's all over, somebody is going to start yelling for his money. Promises don't pay up in a crap game."

"Reckon I could put up something to stake me?"

"What have you got?"

"Now I don't know. Just what you see around, I reckon."

"Land wouldn't do me no good," Semon said. "You can't stick land in your pocket and ride off with it."

Clay looked around. He could neither see nor think of anything he could put up to get into the game. While he was trying to think what to do, Semon rolled the dice methodically, his wrist throwing slowly and surely. He never gave the dice a chance to lie on the ground, but scooped them up the moment they came to a stop. It looked as if he knew what number he was going to throw, and did not take the trouble to see if they rolled as he had thrown them.

"Maybe you've got a watch or something gold in the house," Semon suggested finally, not taking his eyes from the ground under his eyes.

"That's right," Clay cried. "There's a watch in the house. I forgot all about that."

"That won't be enough, though," Semon said. "You've got to have enough to keep your hand in if you lose several times to begin with."

"I couldn't lose it," Clay said.

"Why couldn't you lose it?"

"It belongs to Dene. It's her daddy's watch. He gave it to Dene when he died."

"It don't make no difference to me who's it is or used to be, if you want to play it. The color of money is the same the country over, and watches look all the same to me, if they're gold."

"Oh, it's gold, all right," Clay was quick to assure him. "It's yellowish all over."

"Maybe it is," Semon said.

"I didn't know before that you shot craps, preacher," Tom said. "You act just like nearly everybody else. Most preachers I ever saw wouldn't touch dice with a ten-foot pole."

Semon laughed for the first time since he had started playing with the dice. But even then there was no show of laughter on his face.

"I'm a preacher when I preach, and I'm a sleeper when I sleep."

"And so I reckon you're a gambler when you gamble," Tom nudged him. "That's the thing to do, preacher. I've always said a man ought to act the part of what he claims to be."

"I reckon we'd better start out with a fifty-cent limit and work up," Semon said, getting down closer to the ground on his haunch. The seat of his pants almost touched the hard sand. "I always like to warm the game up slow, to start with, instead of pushing it. It don't do it no good to make it boil before the water's hot."

"That's right, preacher. You know the right way."

Clay came running around the corner of the house, holding the gold watch out in front of him. He was smiling all over his face.

"Here it is," he said excitedly. "Just like I said."

"We'll have to set a value on it, and divide it up," Semon said. "What do you figure it's worth, Tom?"

Tom took the gold watch case and examined it in the sunlight. He shook his head.

"I'll be a dead dog if I know."

"Let me take a look at it," Semon said, reaching for it.

"It aint so very old," Clay said. "Dene's daddy had it I don't know how long before he died, and it still looks bright as new."

Semon held it to his ear and listened. He could hear nothing.

"What's wrong with it?" he asked, and immediately shook it violently. He held it to his ear once more.

"It's been lying on the shelf a long time, hasn't it, Clay?" Tom said.

"No," Clay said. "Dene's been keeping it in her dresser drawer. I had to rummage around under all her clothes just now before I could locate it."

"This thing won't keep time," Semon said, tossing it to Clay. "It won't run a tick. That God-damn watch's no good."

"Maybe it just only needs winding," Clay said. He proceeded to wind the stem, listening closely all the time to hear if it had begun to tick.

"It would be worth about a dollar and a half to me," Semon said. "The gold ought to melt down to that much, anyway."

Clay looked soberly at the watch.

"I thought sure it would fetch more than that."

Semon shook his head determinedly.

"How much did you figure it was worth?" Tom asked.

"Looks like it ought to bring around two dollars, anyhow," Clay said.

"How much?" Semon asked, looking up from the ground.

"I said two dollars."

"Well," Semon said, "maybe it is worth that much. I might have undervalued it a little. I reckon two dollars would be just about right, being as it's gold."

Clay's face beamed. He squatted on his heels, shifting the weight of his body from right to left and back again. He rubbed his hands together warmly after laying the watch between his feet on the sand.

"You're in the watch four times, Horey," Semon said.

"How's that?" Clay asked, looking from one to the other.

"We're playing with a fifty-cent limit, to start with, and so that makes you in the watch four times."

"Aint that a little steep for a poor man? I didn't figure on it being more than two bits, anyhow."

"That's a kid's game," Semon said. "Four bits makes it a man's game, coz."

"I reckon you're bound to be right," Clay agreed. "I hate to be in Dene's daddy's watch only four times, though. It don't look right, somehow."

"Oh, you'll have us all by the hair in no time," Semon told him, getting ready to start the game. He smoothed the sand and wiped off the dice. "You just wait and see if you don't. You'll have me and Tom both by the hair before quits."

Semon took out his money, picking quarters from the handful of change. He placed a stack of eight twenty-five cent pieces at the toe of his right shoe.

"Pitch in, coz," he said. He tossed two of his own quarters into the center of the circle.

Tom laid a half-dollar beside the two quarters. He watched the dice in Semon's hands all the time.

"I'm in the watch four times now," Clay said, laying it carefully on the sand.

"That's right, Horey," Semon told him. "You're in it four times now. We don't want no misunderstanding to crop up later and spoil the game."

He shook the dice in his hands, changing from one hand to the other.

"Get'm hot, preacher!" Tom said. "And if you can't do it, hand them to me."

"I want my four bits' worth covered," Clay said.

"Being as you're visiting, you ought to have the first throw," Semon said, dropping the dice into Tom's hand.

Tom threw another half-dollar on the ground and shook the dice in his cupped hands, holding them high in the air. With a flourish and a grunt he tossed them into the circle. A four and a two came up.

"Can't make it!" Semon said, spitting into his hands and rubbing them together. "He wasn't born to make it!"

"That's my lucky number, folks. Just watch it come up when the old man rolls them."

He threw, and a nine came up.

"He can't make it," Semon said. "He just aint man enough. Watch him crap out!"

Scooping up the dice, Tom clicked them half a dozen times and threw to the circle.

"Huh!" he grunted, and a four and a three came face up under his eyes. "God Almighty!"

"When I say crap out, they can't do nothing else but," Semon said.

Clay looked at the unfamiliar dice in his hand, gently shaking them until they turned over and over.

"The time aint long," he said to himself, shaking the dice with jerky motions of his wrist.

"Hit the dirt!" Semon said as the dice left Clay's hand.

A perfect seven turned up.

"What in hell do you know about that?" Clay asked. He did not expect anyone to answer him. "Now aint that something!" He scooped up the silver coins and patted the gold watch.

"Shoot the two dollars," Clay said, dropping the cash and watch again. "I feel right."

He was covered, but when he finished shooting, he found he was back where he started, with only three-quarters of his watch to bet with.

"We'd better make this game a little more interesting," Semon said, shifting his weight to his left heel and picking up the dice. "I'm in favor of raising bets to a dollar."

Clay was excited now. He was willing, and anxious, to raise the limit. He nodded enthusiastically and squatted lower on the ground.

Semon rolled the dice between his hands, warming them over and over again. When he was ready to throw them, he hurled them heavily to the hard sand. A nine came up. He grinned and scooped the dice.

"Can't beat the old man," he said, blowing the dice and shaking them around his head. "Can't never beat the old man at his own game. I'm a crap shooter from way back yonder, folks!"

"Lucky?" Tom said, watching the dice.

"No, not lucky. Just plain God-damn good at it. I was raised on these before breakfast. I've never forgot how, either."

The dice spun on the sand. The same nine lay on top. There was no way to beat luck like that.

"How much are you in the watch now?" he asked Clay, winking at Tom.

"A dollar," Clay said. "I was in it three times before you shot."

"No, you aren't," Semon shouted angrily, reaching out and covering the watch with his hands. "We raised the limit to a dollar. That makes you only four bits in it now, Horey."

Clay was confused. He had not realized that almost all he owned in the watch had gone, and he could not understand how it went so easily. Reluctantly, he laid it in the ring.

"Just a friendly little game, coz," Semon said. "I wouldn't have hard feelings crop up for no amount of money. When I shoot craps, I like for everybody to feel good, win or lose. That's how I am about it."

"My time's coming," Tom said. "I just aint hit my stride yet."

"If I lose this time, I'm sunk," Clay said dejectedly. "I won't have nothing to put in the pot."

"Don't shuck your corn till the hogs come home," Semon said, counting his money.

After that he threw the dice the second time. He got a five and a six.

"What the hell kind of a game is this, anyhow?" Tom said.

"When I shoot dice, I do just that. Now if you boys want to get your money back, just lay something down to shoot for."

"I'd like to get Dene's daddy's watch back," Clay said, his eyes following it as it was dropped into Semon's pocket.

"You'll have to work for it then, Horey. That's how I got it.

Nobody gets nothing in this world without working like almighty hell."

"How long have you owned those dice?" Tom asked.

"Take a look at them for yourself," Semon offered, throwing him the pair. "I don't want nobody thinking I'd crook a game."

Tom inspected the dice closely, judging the size and weight, but he could find nothing wrong with them. He handed them back to Semon, shaking his head.

"You must just be a lucky-born crap shooter, preacher," he admitted, still shaking his head.

Semon shook the dice and held them poised over his head. He looked down at the ring. Clay felt his eyes upon him.

"Somebody didn't get in this time," Semon stated.

"I'm sticking," Tom said. "That's my dollar bill."

They both looked at Clay.

"I'm cleaned out," he said. "I aint got a cent."

Semon dropped his hand and rolled the dice in the open palm of his hand meditatively.

"Aint in, coz?"

Clay shook his head.

"Aint got nothing else to put up?"

"Not a doggone thing. That watch of Dene's daddy's is all I had."

Semon turned around on his heels, looking in the direction of the barn. His eyes came to rest upon the back end of Clay's automobile under the shed. He jerked his head at the car, and looked around at Clay. Clay's eyes opened wider.

"You can put up your machine, can't you, Horey?"

"Couldn't do that," Clay said firmly.

"Why couldn't you?"

"Doggone it all! That's all I got to ride in!"

"A good crap shooter like you ought not to be scared of losing. I can tell by the way you handle the bones that you are a lucky cuss. Don't be scared, Horey."

"I don't know what Dene would say about it."

"Damn that," Semon said angrily. "It's yours, aint it? If it was mine, I wouldn't stand back because of what some God-damn gyp might say."

Clay looked to Tom. Tom looked at the car, and back at the ground between his feet. He was scared to commit himself.

"Now, I don't know about that," Clay said indecisively.

"Aw, go ahead, Horey. What's not worth risking, aint worth owning, anyway."

"What do you figure it's worth?"

"About fifty dollars like it stands now."

"Fifty dollars!" Clay said, shaking his head. "It's bound to be worth more than that. A heap more than that."

"What makes it bound to be?"

"I've only had it a year now, and I paid four hundred dollars for it in McGuffin."

"They might have cheated you," Semon said, turning once more to inspect the rear end of the automobile.

Clay shook his head. He valued his car at far more than the price Semon had set upon it.

"It's worth a hundred, if it's worth a dime," he said. "I couldn't take less. I'd be cheating myself if I did."

"Well, being as it's you, Horey," Semon said, "I'll say it's worth that. How about you, Tom?"

Tom nodded.

"It's a God-damned sight better than that car of mine out front there," Semon said. "And mine aint hardly worth the junk that's in it. I reckon a hundred for yours wouldn't be any too much to place on it, being as it's you."

Semon took off his coat and rolled up his sleeves. He unloosened his collar and smoothed back his black hair that hung over his forehead like a horse's trimmed mane.

"Let's go," he said. "I'm rearing to go, coz. When I get set shooting crap, I can't be satisfied till the game has run through everything like a dose of salts."

Clay squatted lower on his heels.

"I'm ninety-nine in it," he said. "Is that right?"

"That's right, Horey. Now hold on to your seat. I don't want to have to halt the game while you stop and figure every time how many times you're in the machine. See if you can't keep up with the game."

He warmed the dice in the palms of his hands, shaking them until they clicked like a swiftly running clock. He jerked his hand down, pulling the dice out of the air, and hurled them to the ground with all his might. They all bent forward watching the spinning dice come to a stop on the hard white sand.

"Grab that left ball of yours, Horey!" Semon shouted. "It won't do you no good to pull the right one, because that's the one I'm squeezing."

Chapter XII

CLAY'S shirt and hair were wet with perspiration. The sun was sinking behind the barn, and the shadows were long; but Clay could not keep from sweating. Across from him, only three feet away, Semon Dye looked as cool as the early morning dew.

Semon had said nothing for a long time. He sat lower on his heels, and the seat of his pants scraped the ground each time he moved. He had become accustomed to his position.

Against the brick chimney Tom sat watching them with not a word to say. He had long before lost everything he had with him, and his pockets were empty.

"Looks like something's wrong," Clay said desperately. "It don't look like I ought to lose right straight along as fast as the dice drop."

Semon clicked the dice, shaking them in the cupped palm of his hand, and paid no attention to Clay. He had not even heard what Clay had been saying for the past hour.

Clay was down to his last lone dollar. Semon had been doubling and redoubling. Clay could not understand how a whole hundred dollars could pass out of his hands that fast, and leave nothing behind to show for it. It was more money than he usually cleared on a year's farming.

Semon won the next pot, as usual. There was nothing Clay could do to stop his winning.

"I'm going to give you a chance to win your car back, Horey," Semon told him coldly. "I don't like for any son of a bitch to say that I walked out of the game the winner, and wouldn't give the loser a chance to get even. I'm not that kind of a crap shooter."

"Maybe I'd just better quit," Clay said. "Luck looks like it's against me all around today. I aint never lost like this before in all my life. I've won a little, three or four dollars, and I've lost a little, maybe four or five; but I aint never gone through all I owned before like this."

"It's tough on you, Horey; but you can't argue with the dice. What they say is the way it's meant to be. Aint no use swearing at the dice, either. If you put up a stake, you have got to take your chances of losing as well as winning."

"Maybe I'd do better next time. Looks like it aint no use to keep it up now. I'd only be losing everything in the world."

Semon picked up the dice.

"I want you to have a chance to get even," he insisted. "I can't walk out of a game without giving the loser that last chance at luck."

"I don't want it, though. I aint got a thing left to put up, for one thing. And if I had it, it wouldn't be no use today, because I haven't done a doggone thing but lose all the way through."

"You're going to take it, anyhow," Semon stated, looking at him through the slits of his leather-tight face. "You're going to take that last chance to get even, Horey."

Clay started to get up. He felt a hand pushing him down again. He looked at Semon. Semon's revolver had been pulled from his pocket, and it was laid on the ground between his feet.

"I know when I'm licked," Clay protested.

"You're going to throw the dice one more time, Horey. I'm set on having you take loser's chance to come even."

Clay glanced at Tom, but he could find no help there. Tom lowered his eyes and contemplated the bulldog pistol between Semon's feet, and refused to meet Clay's gaze. He did not wish to take sides in the matter. He was afraid of Semon. After having lost his four dollars, he was through.

"Maybe I would take that last chance," Clay agreed, "but I aint got a thing in the world to put up to stake me. I'm cleaned out—lock, stock, and barrel."

"You can put up this farm. That's a fair bargain against the car, and this thirty or forty dollars, and the watch. Your farm aint worth much more than all that to you. And if you win, everything will be yours, including all this green money. You'd even get your watch back."

"That's Dene's daddy's watch," Clay said.

"I don't give a good God-damn who's it was. It's mine now, and you're going to shake the dice for it."

"I couldn't put up the plowland," Clay said.

"Why couldn't you put it up?"

"The bank in McGuffin holds a mortgage on it."

Semon thought a while. He had not known the place was mortgaged. He had to think quickly.

"You've got one thing more to stake, Horey."

"What's that?"

"Dene," he said, nodding at the weather-beaten side of the house.

Clay laughed, but his laughter turned after a moment to a deep frown. He shook his head.

"No," he said doggedly.

"The hell you say!" Semon shouted. "You'll do it, or I'll blow your God-damn brains to kingdom come!"

He grabbed up the revolver, cocking it with a jerk of his stiff thumb.

"Now, wait a minute, folks," Tom broke in. "Now, just wait a minute."

Semon turned the pistol on Tom. Tom sat down again.

"No sir-ree bob!" Clay said firmly. "Now I know I aint going to throw the dice no more."

Semon pointed the pistol at his head.

"You're going to do it, or the chickens will be around here in another minute pecking at your brains."

"Why, you must be joking, Semon," Clay said frantically. "You don't mean that about making me stake Dene, do you?"

"God damn it, yes!" Semon said, shoving the gun forward. "I mean just what I say, and no more."

"You aint satisfied with just my car and Dene's daddy's watch and Tom's money?"

"You heard me, Horey. I'm telling you to take your chance

of breaking even. This'll be the last throw of the dice. I'll take everything, or nothing. If you win, we'll all lose to you."

"I don't like to dispute you, Semon, but I can't stake Dene."

"All right then, Horey. I've warned you what I'll do if you don't. If you get up from there without throwing the dice, I'll blast your guts to hell and back, and I don't mean maybe."

Clay looked frantically to Tom for help. But there was no help from that quarter. Tom looked afraid to take up for him. He did not have a gun, and Semon did.

"I'll be tickled to death to stake Lorene," Clay said hopefully.

"You can't stake something that don't belong to you. Lorene's not your wife. But Dene is. You've got to stake Dene."

"Why won't Lorene do just as well?"

"I told you why once. She's not your wife. She don't belong to you, but Dene does."

"She used to," Clay said. "That's the same thing. She's my fourth wife."

"Nothing but present wives count in this game. You can't put up something that don't belong to you. Aint that right, Tom?"

They both turned eagerly to Tom. Tom glanced from one to the other; he wished to take up for Clay, but he could not ignore the revolver in Semon's hand. He shook his head.

"I really can't say," he replied. "You folks will just have to fight it out among yourselves. I aint in the game now."

"Aint I right?" Semon insisted, turning the gun upon him.

"Yes, you're right, preacher," Tom said slowly.

"All right now," Semon said, turning back to Clay. "Put her up."

"Go get her?"

"No. Leave her be. Just put her up."

"How can I do that?"

"Say she's in the pot."

"You won't let me put Lorene in there instead?"

"You heard me, you tow-headed son of a bitch! I said put Dene up."

Clay squirmed in his clothes. The perspiration oozed more freely from his skin. Water dripped from his wrists and from the point of his nose.

"What do you aim to do with her if you win her?"

"That wouldn't be none of your God-damn business," Semon said flatly. "That's for me to know."

"You wouldn't take her off with you, would you?"

"I'd do with her as I damned pleased. She'd belong to me then. If you win your car back, wouldn't you do as you pleased with it? Well, I'd do what I wanted to with Dene. She'd be mine."

While they were arguing, Tom reached forward for the dice to examine them more closely than he had the first time. He almost had his hand on them when Semon happened to glance down and see him. Without a moment's hesitation he fired the cocked pistol at Tom's hand. He had not taken good aim, and the bullet missed Tom. Before he had a chance to fire again, Tom jumped back out of the way.

"I swear before God I didn't mean no harm, preacher!" Tom begged.

"If you make another pass for those dice, it'll be your head you'll be reaching for. I'll shoot it off your frame if you make another pass like that."

Tom sank against the chimney, assuring Semon that he would not attempt to get the dice again.

"Those dice don't happen to be loaded, by any chance, do they, preacher?" he said.

Semon glared at him.

"You mind your own business, and I'll mind mine."

He handed the dice to Clay.

"It's your turn," he said. "I wouldn't cheat a man out of his turn when it came due. Shake those dice, Horey, and throw hell out of them."

"For all the stakes?"

"For everything," he replied, nodding.

Clay glanced at the dice in his hand. The weight of them puzzled him, but he did not have the nerve to test them for over-balance. He shook them in his right hand, listening to the click they made when they came together.

"Throw them, Horey," Semon ordered.

"Is Dene in the pot?"

Semon nodded impatiently.

"She's your stake."

"All of her at one time?"

"Everything on one turn of the dice. Winner takes everything there is to take."

He began piling the silver and greenbacks on the ground within the circle.

"I swear to God, I don't want to do this," Clay said desperately.

"Just think how good you'll feel if you win the pot and all the stakes, Horey. Good God, you'll have everything back, and my thirty or forty dollars to boot!"

"I don't care about your money, just so I could have Dene and the car."

"All right then. Throw those dice and see what turns up. Somebody is going to be the winner." A moment later he added: "And somebody is going to be the loser. It always happens like that."

Clay threw the dice on the ground with trembling fingers. When he opened his eyes, an eight lay face up.

"Now, get down and work for it," Semon said. "That's your number. Now, work for it, Horey."

Clay threw the second time. A five turned up. He began to sweat all over again.

"Get those dice hot, Horey," Semon shouted. He was down on his hands and knees, his face only a few inches from the ground.

The next number was a six. Clay's face began to turn white, and the perspiration felt as cold as ice when it trickled down his neck and chest. It made him shiver in the heat.

His hand was raised over his head. He was getting ready to throw the dice for the last time.

"What's my point?" he asked Semon.

"Eight's your point, Horey. Try and make it!"

Clay threw the dice, closing his eyes when they left his hand. He was afraid to look.

There was an interval of silence. Even Semon had not spoken. The dice lay on the hard white sand between them.

"Do you win?" Clay asked weakly.

He opened his eyes for the first time and looked at the circle before him. The number was seven.

"Do I win!" Semon repeated. "Do I win! What the hell is this, anyway? Of course to hell I win! You didn't throw the eight, did you? Well, eight was the point you were trying for. I reckon I do win!"

Clay was on his hands and knees before him.

"What do you aim to do?"

"With what?"

"With the car, and with—with——"

"The first thing I'm going to do is to walk out to that shed yonder and take a look at my new automobile. I've been needing a new car for about a year now. That pile of rattles out there in front of the house will make a good dump for a gully-wash. Drag it out to one of your gullies and heave it in, Horey. It'll keep your plowland from washing away the next time there's a thunder-storm."

Tom got up and moved towards the front yard. He went around the corner of the house and walked hurriedly to his car beside the magnolia tree. He had started the motor and was on his way home before either Clay or Semon had realized it.

Semon replaced the revolver in his pocket. The dice went into his coat pocket. Clay stood watching him, feeling the dead

weight of his hands and arms hanging at his sides. When Semon
had finished brushing his clothes, he walked to the shed beside
the barn. Clay followed in his tracks.

The car he had won from Clay pleased Semon greatly. It
had fairly new tires all around, with a spare just as good; the
paint still held its original gloss and sheen; and the top was in
perfect condition. He got in and started the motor. There was
not a loose bearing to be heard. After listening to the hum for
a while, he got out and pocketed the key.

"I'm much obliged to you, coz," he said, coming out of the
shed. "I'm damned obliged to you. It's a pretty good car for the
money."

Semon walked towards the house. Clay went with him, running beside him with short steps in order to keep up with
Semon's long ones.

When they reached the corner of the house, Clay pulled
Semon's arm. They stopped, facing each other, and Semon bent
down to look into Clay's eyes.

"What do you want, Horey?"

"What do you aim to do now?"

"Nothing. Why?"

"Aiming to go in the house?"

"Maybe, and maybe not. I haven't decided yet."

"You aint going in the room where Dene is, are you?"

"Calm down, Horey. Calm down."

"Now, Dene is my wife, and——"

"Well, what's that to me?"

"Well, Dene is my wife, now, and I'll be doggone if I want

to have you thinking I'm going to let you claim her. Now, I aint going to stand for it. I wouldn't be mean about it—I'm just telling you to stop where you are, if that's what you're aiming at."

"Don't come whining around me, Horey," Semon said sharply, shoving Clay away with a sweep of his hand. "You lost, and I won. There's nothing more to the story."

"Now, you ought to be satisfied with taking Lorene. You take her, if you want somebody. I don't care if you do take her. But you aint going to do nothing with Dene."

"Just one more whine like that, Horey, and I'll blow your brains all over creation."

"Those dice of yours don't happen to be loaded, do they?"

"These are my dice, and I don't have to tell you anything about them. You got in the game by walking in unasked; now walk yourself out, and stay out. I've heard enough of your whining."

They went up the porch steps and through the hall together. Semon looked through each door as they passed. When they got to Clay and Dene's room, Semon stopped and looked in at Lorene and Dene. He smiled, waved his hand at them, and strode inside.

"Maybe you'd better tell her, Horey, so she'll believe it right off," he said to Clay. "Go ahead and tell her."

Clay sat down in a chair, wiping the perspiration from his face.

"Go ahead, or I'll have to do it myself," Semon urged.

"We had a little crap game out in the yard, Dene," he began.

"The three of us—Semon, Tom, and me. Semon cleaned us out. I had to put up the car, and I lost that. Then Semon made me——"

"Don't stop," Semon said.

"Semon made me put up you, and I lost again."

Lorene was on her feet in an instant.

"You're a dirty son of a bitch, Semon Dye!" she screamed at him. "You're a low-down crook!"

Semon laughed at her.

"It was a fair game of craps," he said slowly. "Clay took just as much of a chance of winning as he did of losing. The only thing is, he lost and I won. That's the way gambling goes."

"But you aint going to take her!" Clay shouted at him, jumping to his feet. "Now you just try and see if you can!"

Semon jerked out his revolver and aimed it at Clay. Before he could pull the trigger, his arm was jerked down by Lorene. When he raised it again to fire the second time, she fought him tooth and nail, biting into his arm and scratching the backs of his hands. He yelled with pain, dropping the gun. He tried to kick her, but she clung to him.

There was plenty of time for Clay to reach the pistol on the floor at Semon's feet, but instead of getting it, he ran to the other side of the room where Dene was. He grabbed her by the arm and was pulling her through the door when he heard Semon's shout. Semon ordered him to stop where he was.

Clay turned back and saw Semon pick up the pistol and hit Lorene on the head with the butt. She fell at his feet unconscious.

"Come on back in here," Semon said. "I aimed to handle this in a peaceful way, but it looks like you sons of bitches here won't act like white people. Now, get back over there, and don't make a move towards me."

Clay went back as Semon had ordered him, and Dene clung to his arm.

"You get in that corner, Horey," Semon said, "and stay there till I tell you to come out."

After Clay had obeyed him, Semon laid the pistol on the table and picked Lorene up and carried her to the bed.

"Now, when you people decide to act like white folks, just let me know, and I'll let you alone. I'd hate to have to shoot some of you when there really's not a bit of need of it. So just make up your minds to act natural, and it'll be all right by me."

No one spoke in reply, and Semon went to the bed and sat down. He looked at Lorene a moment. She was breathing heavily, and her eyelids had begun to flutter. He watched her calmly while she slowly regained consciousness.

Lorene turned over and opened her eyes. She did not know where she was for several minutes, and when she did recognize the room, she could not remember what had happened.

Over in the opposite corner, Clay had become more calm. The perspiration had dried on his face and chest, and his head no longer felt hot.

"I'll make a bargain with you, Semon," he said slowly, prolonging each word.

"How's that?" Semon asked, looking up from Lorene.

"I'll go in debt to get her back—to have Dene back, I mean."

"In which way is that?" Semon asked, interested in the proposal.

Clay walked across the room and stood in front of him.

"I'll go to town and borrow some money to buy her away from you, if you'll leave her alone now."

Semon jumped to his feet and looked down at Clay.

"How much can you borrow?"

"I might could get hold of a hundred dollars on next year's crop."

Semon slipped the revolver into his pocket.

"Reckon you could rake together that much?"

"I can try," Clay said eagerly.

"All right," Semon agreed. "That's a bargain. You get a hundred dollars and hand it over to me before tomorrow night, and I'll give her back to you. That's a fair enough trade for me."

Clay clutched his arm.

"You're not lying to me, are you? Is that the truth you say?"

"I swear before the living God, Horey."

Clay ran to the door. He did not stop to look back at Dene in his haste.

"Where are you going?" Semon called after him, following him to the hall.

Clay did not stop to answer. He ran across the porch and down the back steps.

"I'm going to McGuffin to get the money," he yelled back at Semon.

Chapter XIII

AFTER supper that night Lorene took the bottle of medicine from the kitchen shelf and went down to Susan's. She intended instructing Susan to give Vearl several doses of it every day, and to see that Vearl was taken to the doctor in McGuffin after she left. Lorene knew she could depend upon the woman to remind Clay until he would take Vearl. She had already planned to leave Monday morning for Jacksonville with Semon.

Semon and Dene were alone in the house. At first Dene was afraid to look at him; but later, after he had spoken so tenderly to her, she was no longer shy. Semon made her feel, for the first time in her life, like a lady.

"I'd like to speak to you about your soul, Dene," he said first. "You can talk freely to me, knowing who I am. I'm a man of God, Dene."

Dene hung her head to hide the flush that came to her face. She did not know what to say. After he had finished speaking, she noticed for the first time that there was a tingling in her body; the sensation frightened her.

"Speak, Dene," he urged, moving his chair to her side. "Don't be afraid to unburden your soul in the presence of a man of God."

"I've always tried to do right," she said. "I don't want to be bad."

"We are all wicked, Dene. There isn't a man or woman in the world who isn't wicked. But I know you don't want to be. That's why I've offered to help you. I want to help you. You can trust me, because I'm here to help you."

"Would it be all right for me to tell you?"

"Now, Dene, don't be afraid. What you tell me goes no further than me and God. It will do your soul good to tell me what's troubling you."

"It didn't trouble me any until you came. But now I feel like I've been the baddest thing."

"That's your conscience hurting you, Dene. You'll never be happy again until you come right out with it and tell me everything."

"I've always tried to be good," she said softly. "My mother taught me to be good and to believe in God. She said I ought never let the devil tempt me."

"What kind of temptation was that, Dene?"

"She said it was wicked to love Clay before we got married."

Semon leaned back and thought a moment, holding his chin in his hand.

"That's bad, Dene. It's very bad."

"But that's not everything, Mr. Dye," she said quickly. "There's a lot more I haven't told you yet."

"More?" he said. "You've been even more sinful than that, Dene?"

"Yes, sir," she said.

"Do you mean to say you sinned more times than that?"

"Yes, sir. I was wicked another time, too."

Semon jerked his chair closer and took her hands in his. He patted her softly, stroking her hands and arms with his huge palm and fingers. She tried to draw away from him at first, but he shook his head.

"I want you to tell me what it is, Dene. I have a right to know. I'm a man of God. I came here to help you. You must tell me all about yourself before it's too late. If you should die tomorrow, you'd go straight to hell as sure as the world you live on. But after you tell me, why, you won't have to worry any more."

"Oh, I want so much to tell you everything, Mr. Dye. I'm not used to talking to men, except to Clay, and I'm a little scared. But you are a preacher, and I know I can tell you. I'm the baddest thing."

He stroked her arms from wrists to shoulders, rubbing the rough skin of his fingers up and down her tender flesh.

"Now, Dene, you'll have to tell me the truth about what I'm going to ask you. Only the truth will serve. If you lie to me, the Lord will damn you to everlasting hell. Are you willing to tell me the truth, Dene? Now, remember, I'm not asking this as a man. It's as the preacher that I am that I must have a truthful answer."

"I'll tell you the truth about everything, Mr. Dye. I want so much to tell it. I know I'll never be able to sleep again at night if I don't tell you. I've got to tell you!"

"Dene, is Clay Horey the only man you've ever had private dealings with? Don't forget now—you must not lie to me. I'm a man of God, I am."

"What kind of dealings do you mean?"

"We'll have to speak plainly about this thing, Dene. I must ask you plainly, and you must answer me plainly. Don't be afraid, because God is waiting to hear you."

"I'll tell you, Mr. Dye!"

"Have you ever admitted any other man besides Clay Horey?"

"You mean—to me?"

"I mean to you. That's exactly what I mean."

She turned away from Semon and tried to look across the room. She was silent for such a long time that Semon thought she had refused to answer him. He took both of her arms in his hands and pulled her around to face him. Once more, and slowly, he began to stroke her bare arms.

"Once," she whispered, looking down at the floor.

"How come just once, Dene?"

"He only asked me once, Mr. Dye."

"Why didn't the son of a bitch ask you more? What was wrong, Dene?"

Semon trembled with anger.

"He was scared, Mr. Dye."

"Scared of who? Scared of what?"

"He was scared of Clay.—And because I was a white girl."

Semon jerked her painfully.

"Wasn't he a white man himself?"

"No," Dene said.

Semon jumped to his feet, pulling her with him. When they stumbled over one of the chairs, he kicked it with all his might across the room. Then he put his arms around her and held her tightly while he stroked her buttocks with his rough hands.

After a while he drew her head upward and looked down into her eyes. Dene's head lay against his chest, and she had to look straight upward before she could see his face.

"It was a nigger, Dene?" he asked. "You got down and let a nigger have you?"

"I couldn't help it, Mr. Dye! I just couldn't!"

"Why couldn't you? You could run away, couldn't you?"

"I didn't want to run away, though," she said, drawing her head down and laying it against his chest. "I wanted him to do it."

"You loved a nigger," he said, looking down at her.

"Yes," she said. "I liked him."

Semon continued to hold her tightly in his arms. Once, when she tried to slip away, he crushed her more ruthlessly against his body.

"This is serious, Dene. It's very serious. I don't know what God is going to do to you about it. But I'll pray for you, and you must pray too. Some day He will forgive you. He always forgives folks who repent. But it's serious just the same. This thing of white girls laying down with darkies ought to stop. It looks like it gets worse and worse all the time, though. I've had a lot of trouble about that. The girls seem to think that darkies are better than white men, or something. I don't know what it is. White girls and women tell me that they just didn't want to stop living with darkies, once they started. They all know it's wrong, but they can't or won't stop it even to save their souls from hell. I don't know what's going to be done about it. The law won't help none, because nobody pays any attention to it. It looks to me like a white girl ought to want to stick to her own color. There's enough yellow darkies in the country now, and there's more and more born every day. Pretty soon everybody will be the same yellowish color if this keeps up."

Dene had begun to cry, and she tried even harder to get away from Semon. She wished to run and hide from him so he could not see her again. She knew she had committed a sin. She was convinced that it was the worst sin she could have committed.

"You must tell me all about it, Dene," he said. "You can't stop without finishing. God wouldn't like that."

He sat down in the chair and pulled her to him. For a while she stood in front of him, held firmly in the vise of his outspread legs. She did not know he was placing her on his lap until she opened her eyes and saw him lift her and place her solidly upon him. He held one arm around her waist and the other around her legs so she could not spring up and run away.

"It was Hardy," she cried. "I let him know he could have me. He wouldn't do it then, but I wouldn't let him go. I locked the door and wouldn't let him out. Then I let him know that he had to. He was afraid, but I made him stay."

"Hardy!" Semon said deep down in his throat.

"Yes, Hardy Walker! He took me in here one day right after dinner. Clay had gone to the field, but I didn't care if he did come back. I had to have Hardy. He held me tight when I went to him. He was still afraid, but I made him want to. If he had stopped, I'd have gone crazy. I just had to have him, and I didn't care what happened. I loved Clay, and I still love him, but I just couldn't help having Hardy. He wasn't a darky then. He was a man. And he was the best man I'd ever had. That's why I couldn't let him stop. It was the strangest thing."

Semon was speechless for several minutes after she had finished. He had heard confessions from women before, but not one of them had ever been anything like that. Dene had told him what other girls and women had held back.

She cried louder. She tried to get out of his arms, but Semon would not let her. He held her around the waist and legs more strongly than ever.

Suddenly she screamed in his ears.

"You made me tell you!"

"Confession is good for the soul, Dene," he said at once.

He drew her closer and kissed her cheeks and neck and, finally, her lips. When he released her, she did not move. After a while he raised her head and looked at her, and she did not know whether to cry or to laugh. He kissed her again, and after that she offered her lips in return.

"I think I can save you, Dene," he said hoarsely.

She closed her eyes and lay her head on his shoulder.

"I'm going to save you. I won't let you be damned."

Her lips parted as if to answer him, but no sound reached his ears.

"I'm going away Monday morning, and I want you to go with me to work for the Lord. That's the only way to be saved now, Dene."

"I love the Lord," she said excitedly.

"You'll be one of his angels."

"Oh, I love the Lord so much it hurts!"

"Praise God!" he said, kissing her.

When he lifted her to her feet and stood up beside her, she held to him frantically. He led her across the room and laid her on the bed. She lay with unopened eyes while he put his arms around her and kissed her hungrily.

"We'll leave Monday morning," he said again. "Be ready to leave early, Dene. You must work for the Lord now if you are going to be saved. I'll pray for you all the time."

"I love the Lord!"

Semon laid his revolver on the table by the bed and blew out the light. He came back, kneeling at the bed, and found her lips with his.

Her body trembled as he took her in his arms and stroked her with his hands.

"Don't be afraid of me, Dene," he said hoarsely. "I won't hurt you. I'm a man of God, I am."

He pressed his face against her breasts and kissed her savagely. When she could wait no longer, she threw her arms around his head, crying hysterically.

"I love the Lord!" she screamed in the dark room.

Chapter XIV

CLAY got back home the next morning a little before nine o'clock. He had been whipping the mule with a hickory switch all the way from McGuffin, but the mule still refused to go faster than a walk. The animal was fresh and unharried; Clay was worn to a frazzle.

He could see Semon sitting on the front porch when he was a quarter of a mile away. It was then that the mule slowed down even more, instead of walking faster at the sight of the barn, and Clay threw himself to the road and ran the rest of the way home. He left the mule to come alone.

No one came out to meet him, but he was too excited to notice it.

"Here it is!" he shouted, waving a handful of greenbacks high above his head.

Semon had forgotten what Clay had gone to town for, but when he saw the money, he remembered all about it.

"I got it," Clay said, running up the steps. "Every penny of it. I'm ready to pay it over, Semon."

"Where'd you get it?" Semon asked suspiciously, reaching in the air for Clay's hand and pulling it closer.

"Where?"

"Yes, where? I don't intend taking stolen money and get myself locked up in one of these little back-country calabooses. You didn't rob a store or bank to get it, did you?"

"I sure didn't," Clay said, too excited to sit down or to stand still. "I borrowed it at the farmers' warehouse against next year's cotton crop. I signed my name for it. I wouldn't steal money."

Still holding Clay's wrist, Semon tried to take the money with his other hand. Clay hastily jerked it beyond his reach.

"Now just hold on a minute," he said, shaking his head. "Just paying over the money aint good business. I know it aint. You've got to say you release me from all debts, and turn Dene back over to me. That's a fair way of doing things."

"Can't you trust a man of God?"

"Just look here a minute," Clay said. "Now I want to know exactly what kind of a preacher you are. I asked some folks in McGuffin about it, and they said they'd heard a heap about you, but hadn't ever run across you. When I told them how you've been carrying on out here in Rocky Comfort, first with Sugar, and then sopping up corn liquor, and now shooting dice, they said you sounded like the damnedest kind of preacher they'd ever heard tell about. I told them you was a real traveling preacher, but I couldn't hardly convince most of them of it."

"You don't doubt my word, do you, coz?"

"Me? I can't say. It was the other folks who said that about you. But just what kind of a preacher be you, anyway?"

"God called me to preach to sinners," Semon said gravely. "That's all the explaining I ever have to do to white people. If folks don't take my word for it, then I know the devil is in them."

Clay drew up a chair, holding the money tightly in his fist. He looked at it closely, his eyes blinking at the sight of so many soiled green notes.

"Are you still aiming to preach at the schoolhouse Sunday?" he said, turning to Semon.

"I am, I am," Semon said solemnly. "That's what the Lord told me to come back over here to Georgia for. I wouldn't be sitting here now if He hadn't told me to make haste and come."

"I'll be doggone if you don't hang on, as a fellow said, till there aint no knowing about you. I never did see a man just keep on and on like you do."

"What do you mean to say by that?"

"You've got a nearly brand-new car, and Dene's daddy's watch, and this hundred dollars I'm bound to give you, and I can't see why you don't go on off to the next place now."

"I'm going to preach Sunday," Semon said doggedly. "Can't nothing, hell or high water, stop me from doing that. I came over here to save sinners, and I'm going to save them if I have to get down and come through with them myself."

"Well, here it is," Clay said, reluctantly handing over the greenbacks. "And I reckon you'll say you aint got a hold on Dene now."

"Me?" Semon said. He grabbed the money and started in at once to count it.

"Yes, you," Clay said bitterly. "I'm getting a little doggone tired of having you around here. If I've got to get my religion from you, I don't care now whether I get none or not."

"Now that's no way to talk, Horey," Semon said, stopping to look at Clay. He held the money between his fingers where he had stopped counting. "You act like I done something mean to you."

"It aint that so much as it's something else. I aint convinced that you are a preacher."

"The Lord heard you then."

"He did, sure enough?"

"He sure did. You want to be careful of what you say."

Clay thought for several minutes. He looked across the yard towards the woods where Rocky Comfort Creek was hidden.

"But you aint a reverend, are you?" Clay asked.

"No," Semon said. "I aint. I leave that to other people who crave to be called that."

"Then what kind of a preacher be you, anyway?"

"I'm a lay preacher."

"You are?"

"Yes, I'm that kind."

"Is that any different than the real kind?"

"What real kind?"

"The reverend kind."

"Those kind of preachers aint a bit more privy to the Lord than I am. I take my living where I can find it, and those other kind stick to one place all the time. That's all the difference there is. And with the Lord there's no difference at all. All of us are preachers in His sight. I don't take no back-water from any kind of preacher, reverend or lay."

"I reckon you're resting up today to do some powerful preaching at the schoolhouse tomorrow," Clay said. "I wouldn't miss that session for nothing in the world. I always said I'd like to be on the ground to see a preacher make the devil take to his heels. I reckon that's what you're aiming to do tomorrow."

"I always give the devil a licking," Semon said. "Not only tomorrow, but every time I preach I bear down on him till he hollers for the calf-rope. And he'll holler for it tomorrow, too."

"Maybe you'll drive the devil clear out of Rocky Comfort. That would be a fine thing to do. The folks here has always had a little of the devil in them. Looks like they just try to see how wicked they can be. You will have to do some tall preaching to get them to shed their ways."

"The people here are no different than the folks all over the country. The devil is everywhere in Georgia. No matter where it is you go, you see his shiny head sticking up."

"Has the devil got a shiny head?" Clay asked.

"Has he! Just like a bald head slicked with lard."

"You don't say!"

"And it's red, too."

"Well, I'll be doggone! I never knew that before. I somehow had the idea that the devil looked something like—well, to tell you the honest-to-God truth, Semon, I didn't know what he looked like."

Semon had finished counting the money by then. He held

it in his hand, looking at it, shaking it, and feeling it with his fingers. It was with reluctance that he put it into his pocket out of sight.

"Maybe we'd better ride up to the schoolhouse and let you look over the ground," Clay suggested. "You can see the lay of the land, and you'll know what to look for tomorrow."

"That's fine. I would like to see it. I haven't been no further away than Tom Rhodes' since I got here last Wednesday afternoon."

"I reckon we can ride up in the automobile," Clay said, leading the way to the shed.

"Sure," Semon said. "We can ride in my car."

He got in, found the key he had put in his pocket, and started the engine. Clay sat down beside him in the front seat, holding the door partly open, and keeping one foot on the runningboard.

Semon operated the car with no trouble at all. He backed it out, drove it out of the yard, and turned up the road just as if he had been in the habit of driving it for two or three years. They had nothing to say to each other.

A hundred yards from Tom Rhodes's house Semon slowed down. He looked at the house and barn and at the outhouses scattered around the place without design.

"What's the matter now?" Clay asked, following his eyes, and feeling the car slow down.

"It might not be a bad idea to stop and speak to Tom," Semon said. "I haven't seen him since yesterday."

Without waiting for Clay to reply, he turned into the driveway and drove down to the barnyard gate. He stopped the car, pocketed the key, and got out.

"Now I don't know where Tom might be," Clay said, walking towards the barn. "Sometimes he goes to town on Saturday, and sometimes he don't."

"There's his car in the shed. He ought to be around somewhere."

The Negro who worked around the house and barn came out of an outhouse.

"Where's Mr. Tom?" Clay asked.

"Down in the pasture," Frank said, pointing beyond the garden and orchard. "You can find him down there."

They climbed the barnyard fence at the gate and walked across the garden. The vegetables were up and growing well. Semon stopped and pulled up a carrot. After wiping the soil off with his hands, he began eating it, taking big bites one after the other and crunching the pulp in his jaws.

Tom was nowhere to be seen in the pasture, but there was a cow shed near the creek. They went towards it, stepping gingerly along the crooked cow path.

At the door Clay stopped and looked inside. There was Tom, perched on a stool, looking through a crack in the wall of the shed. He had not seen them.

"What in thunder are you doing peeping through that crack, Tom?" Clay said, stepping inside and stopping to look closely at Tom.

Tom jumped to his feet, his face suddenly red. He did not know what to do to hide his embarrassment.

"Nothing," he said, trying to laugh.

Semon went across the shed and bent over at the crack. He peered through it for a few minutes, shutting one eye and squinting the other.

"I don't see a thing but the woods over there," Semon said, standing erect and looking at Tom. But he was still wondering what it was that could be seen through the crack.

Tom did not try to explain.

"What in thunderation's going on over across there, Tom?" Clay asked. He bent over and looked through the crack in the wall. He shut one eye, squinted the other one, but he could still see nothing except the pine trees.

"Is somebody over there, Tom?" Semon asked.

Tom shook his head, trying not to meet the eyes of either of them.

"I just come down here sometime and sit," he said, hemming and hawing. "I don't have much else to do, so I just sit and look through the crack. It used to be that I could find plenty to do, but I've got so I'd rather stay down here."

"And look at nothing?" Semon asked in amazement.

"Well, there's nothing but the woods over there, I reckon. There's that, and something else. I don't know what."

"I'll be doggone," Clay said. "I never knew you did that before. There aint much sense in doing it, is there, Tom?"

"No," Tom said. "I don't reckon there's a bit of sense in it. But I just do it, anyway."

Semon sat down on one of the stools. He then saw the jug that had been sitting all that time against the wall.

"I reckon you're going to be neighborly with the jug, won't you, Tom?" he said.

"That's what it's for. Just help yourself."

Semon took a long draft of the corn whisky and set the jug down none too lightly. There was no floor under the shed, only the bare earth, and so it did not break. He passed the back of his hand across his mouth and licked it.

"Help yourself, Clay," Tom said. "That's what I make it for. Wouldn't be no sense in running it off if nobody made use of it."

While Clay and Tom were drinking from the jug, Semon moved over to the stool by the wall and bent his head against the crack. He sat there, looking through it with his eye squinted for several minutes. After that he raised his head and looked at the others rather sheepishly.

"See anything?" Clay said.

"Not much."

"Move over, then, and let me take a look through it."

Clay sat down and looked through the crack. There was nothing much to be seen except the trees on the other side of the pasture. The fence over there that bordered that side of the pasture was barbed wire, and the posts were split pine. He saw all that in a glance, and there was nothing else to see, but he continued to look through the crack as though he saw something that he had never seen before in his life.

"Where you folks headed for?" Tom asked Semon.

"To the schoolhouse. That's where we started. I don't reckon there's much up there to see, though."

"No," Tom said, moving restlessly on his stool. "No, there aint much up there. Least, I never could see much up around there."

He turned around to see if Clay had finished looking through the crack. After waiting as long as he could, he got up and went over there.

"What's the matter?" Clay asked.

"It's about my turn now."

He pushed Clay away from the stool and sat down to press his face against the wall where the crack was. He moved his head slightly to the left, then lowered it a fraction of an inch. After that he sat motionless.

"See anything, coz?" Semon said.

Tom said nothing.

"I reckon I'll take my other drink now, instead of later," Semon said. He picked up the jug and drank heavily.

After he had finished, he handed it over to Clay.

"There wouldn't be much sense in going to the schoolhouse now," Semon said, shaking his head at Clay. "There's nothing much up there to go for."

"It's bound to be just like it was the last time I saw it," Tom agreed.

Semon walked nervously around the cow shed. He came to a stop beside Tom.

"Don't hog it all the time, coz," he said, pushing him. "Let a white man take a look once in a while."

Tom got up and looked for the jug.

"I can't seem to remember when I liked to look at a thing

so much as I do now," Semon said, adjusting his eye to the crack.

Clay leaned against the wall, taking out his harmonica. He tapped the flakes of tobacco and weed out of it, and drew it swiftly across his mouth. It made a sound like an automobile tire going flat.

He started playing "I've Got a Gal."

Semon, with his eye glued to the crack, began keeping time with his feet on the bare earth.

"That's the God-damnedest little slit in the whole world," Tom said. "I come down here and sit on the stool and look through it all morning sometimes. There's not a doggone thing to see but the trees over there, and maybe the fence posts, but I can't keep from looking to save my soul. It's the doggonest thing I ever saw in all my life."

Semon settled himself more comfortably on the stool.

"There's not a single thing to see," Tom said, "and then again there's the whole world to look at. Looking through the side of the shed aint like nothing else I can think of. You sit there a while, and the first thing you know, you can't get away from it. It gets a hold on a man like nothing else does. You sit there, screwing up your eye and looking at the trees or something, and you might start to thinking what a fool thing you're doing, but you don't give a cuss about that. All you care for is staying there and looking."

Semon continued keeping time to the harmonica with both feet. Neither of them made any sound on the bare ground, but he kept it up just the same.

"She wore a little yellow dress——"

Clay was playing as though his life depended upon it, and Tom was singing a line every once in a while. He hummed under his breath when he was not singing.

Semon was reaching for the glass jug. His hand was searching in a circle for it, but it was beyond his reach. He would not stop looking through the crack for even a second to see where the jug really was.

"Can't help you out none, preacher," Tom said. "You'll have to come and get it. It's my time to look some now."

"—those eyes were made for me to see."

Tom sang a line, and stopped to talk again.

"You ought to give somebody else a chance to look, every once in a while, preacher."

Semon got up from the stool without moving his head. He stood there bent over until Tom shoved him out of his way.

"In the night-time is the right time——"

"Shove off, preacher," Tom said, giving him a final push.

Semon sat down on the other stool, rubbing the strain from his left eye. He blinked several times, resuming the tapping of his feet.

He took a long drink and put the jug down at Clay's side.

"That's the God-damnedest slit I ever saw in all my life," Semon said. "You can look through there all day and never get tired. And come back the next day, and I'll bet it would look just as good. There's something about looking through a crack that nothing else in the whole wide world will give you."

Clay had warmed up until he could not stop. The song he

was playing had long before run out, but the chorus would not end. He could not make himself quit.

Finally the harmonica filled up, and he had to stop. He was sorry the song was over.

Tom was still humming the tune, though, and he ended up with another line from the chorus.

"Coz, do that some more," Semon said. "I want to hear that piece again. I don't reckon I've ever heard a mouth-organ play a prettier one."

"It's my time to look through the crack now."

"Here, take another drink, and me and Tom will give you the next two turns, instead of one. Just go ahead and play that pretty little piece some more. It makes me want to cry, it's that good, and I feel like crying over it now."

Clay drank, and jerked the harmonica across his lips. It sounded this time like air going into a tire.

With his head pressed tightly against the shed wall, Tom started humming again. He patted his feet on the ground, swinging into rhythm with the tune Clay was playing.

"There's never been but one gal like that in all the world," Semon said. The tears welled in his eyes and dripped against the backs of his hands. "If I could just look through the crack and see her, I wouldn't ask to live no longer. That crack is the God-damnedest thing I ever looked through. I sit there and look, and think about that gal, thinking maybe I'll see her with the next bat of my eye, and all the time I'm looking clear to the back side of heaven."

He strode to the wall and pushed Tom away. Without waiting to sit down first, he pressed his eye to the slit in the wall. After that he slowly sat down on the stool.

"—*you're the prettiest one and the sweetest one.*"

Tom stooped and picked up the jug. He took his drink and replaced it at Clay's feet. Clay was too busy then to stop for a drink. He could not stop.

"*When I'm loving you, I'm telling you——*"

Semon put his hand to his face and wiped the tears from his cheeks.

"I don't know what I'd do without that crack in the wall," Tom said. "I reckon I'd just dry up and die away, I'd be that sad about it. I come down here and sit and look, and I don't see nothing you can't see better from the outside, but that don't make a bit of difference. It's sitting there looking through the crack at the trees all day long that sort of gets me. I don't know what it is, and it might not be nothing at all when you figure it out. But it's not the knowing about it, anyway—it's just the sitting there and looking through it that sort of makes me feel like heaven can't be so doggone far away."

Chapter XV

~~~~~~

NEARLY everyone in Rocky Comfort was on the school-house grounds at two o'clock Sunday afternoon. Some of the families living on the other side of Rocky Comfort Creek had started out early that morning in wagons pulled by slow-walking mules. They forded the creek a hundred yards above the schoolhouse and drove up sitting in house chairs that had been placed in the wagon-bed. Others came in cars. Many walked, and some rode mule-back.

Clay Horey and Dene, together with Semon and Lorene, had arrived at one o'clock. They had been the first there, and Clay and Semon went inside and opened up the building and got things ready for the services. It was a two-room school, and the larger room had about forty desks in it. At one end of the room there was a platform, where the teacher sat, and on it two chairs and a table.

While they were inside, Lorene and Dene went down to the spring for a drink of water. They were gone for nearly half an hour.

The schoolhouse grounds soon filled with teams and wagons,

~~~~~~

and bare-back mules tied to trees. The automobiles were left in the sandy clearing between the building and the grove. There were thirty or forty persons there, not counting the younger children and babies.

Semon and Clay came out the front door and surveyed the crowd.

"Looks like the people are starved for preaching," Semon said, his eyes sweeping over the grounds. "The Lord sure did know what He was doing when He told me to come to Rocky Comfort. These people are ripe for religion. Saving them will be as easy as falling off a log."

"Shucks," Clay said, laughing a little, "that's nothing. Folks in Rocky Comfort will go anywhere anytime when there's something going on. It don't matter much to them whether it's a wedding or a funeral, or even just an old-fashioned country break-down."

"A break-down?" Semon asked.

"Sure."

"I'll have to remember to say something against dancing," he said, making a quick note in his mind. "That's always a good subject to preach about to country people."

He walked off into the groups of people, shaking hands and introducing himself. The men shook hands with him readily enough, almost eagerly; but the women and girls were slow to touch his hand, and they looked at him in quick glances. Semon knew how to make himself at ease in a group of women, though; and, moreover, he had a way with them that won their interest. Soon they were all laughing and crowding around him.

"The preacher's been staying at your house, aint he, Clay?" Ralph Stone said.

"He's been there since last Wednesday," Clay told him proudly. Some of the men pressed closer to hear them talk about Semon. "I reckon it's something to puff up about when the preacher comes and stays at a man's house that long."

"Ever see him before?" Ralph asked.

"Never laid eyes on him before last Wednesday when he drove up and lit."

Another man pushed through the crowd surrounding Clay and Ralph Stone.

"The preacher's a sport among the women, aint he, Clay? Just look at him step around over there. He's got all the girls giggling like they had been goosed."

Everybody turned and looked at Semon. He was laughing and joking with the women and girls, stopping every now and then to stoop over a toddling baby and chuck it under the chin.

"The women take to anybody who makes out he's a fool about them and the young ones," Ralph said. "You can't tell them no different, after that. You just have to let him run his course, like a dose of castor oil. There aint no way in heaven or hell of stopping what's bound to be."

Semon was moving towards the schoolhouse door. When he got to the steps, he stopped and waved his arms above his head and called the people to come inside. The men made no move; and the women waited until Semon had entered the building, and then they all crowded in at the same time, like a flock of sheep all trying to jump through a gap in a fence.

"I don't know what he can find to preach about that everybody in Rocky Comfort don't already know something about," Ralph said. "I figure that he'll preach just like all the traveling preachers who've been through here since I was a boy."

Tom Rhodes came up the path from the spring and went to his car. He had been waiting down at the creek bank until his wife had gone into the schoolhouse.

The other men and older boys went further into the grove and sat down in a wide circle, some leaning back against trees, others perching on their heels, and looked at each other with familiar nods of the head.

"Come here a minute, Clay," Tom said under his breath, standing behind Clay. "Want to take a little walk?"

Clay nodded and left the circle. He followed Tom to his car and helped him take out the jug from the back seat. The jug had been wrapped in a burlap bag and hidden there.

They strolled out of sight and stood behind some pine trees drinking Tom's corn whisky. They made the cork tight when they had enough, and covered the jug with pine needles where it could be picked up later in the day.

When they came back to the clearing, they could hear a humming sound in the schoolhouse. The women were doing their best to raise a tune without even so much as a fiddle. Semon had taken out his tuningfork and had struck it on the table several times. The note came all right, but he could not keep the pitch. The girls and women were timid about singing, and the song never became loud enough to be heard on the outside where the men were.

Down the path towards the spring, two boys were thrashing about on the ground, striking each other with their fists. The other boys had taken sides and were urging the two scrappers to keep up the fight. The men heard what was taking place, but they paid no attention to it. They went on whittling and chewing, and listening to the discussion between Ralph Stone and Jack Rainwater about the right time of the month to plant corn.

Every once in a while one of the girls or women would come out of the schoolhouse carrying a bawling baby who refused to be quieted while Semon was preaching. After the baby had been taken out into the grove to play a while, it was carried back inside again.

"I sure would like to hear Semon preach," Tom said. He sat down in the circle and rested himself on his heels. "I don't know what he's got to say that I don't already know, but I'd just like to hear him, anyway."

The others stopped talking to listen to Tom Rhodes.

"There aint no law against going in the schoolhouse and cocking your ear to him, Tom," somebody said.

"There aint no law, but I can't make myself go in there in the broad daylight. I reckon I'll just have to wait for night and go in with everybody else."

"He won't get warmed up till about eight o'clock tonight," Ralph said. "It'd just be a waste of time sitting in there while he's still cold. I've seen traveling preachers before, and none of them can get good and hot under the collar till about half an hour after night-fall. It takes the blackness of night to make a preacher cut loose with all he's got and do real old-fashioned preaching."

Somebody was listlessly tossing a pair of battered dice on the ground. He did not take much interest in what he was doing, and he had not even taken the trouble to clear the pine needles away. Unless someone was willing to stake a few dimes, there was not much incentive in merely throwing dice on the ground to see what number turned up. It was too early in the afternoon to start a game, anyway.

Semon's voice suddenly broke through the quiet air and beat against their ears. No one could understand then what he was saying, at that distance, but it sounded as if he were shouting at someone who had made him angry. Everybody turned and listened.

Inside the schoolhouse the crowd of women and girls sat motionlessly behind their desks listening to Semon Dye. He tore the air with his blasts. He waved his arms and shook his fists in the face of an imaginary devil, and at the end of each pause he emphasized his message by pounding on the teacher's table beside him.

"You all ought to stop it! It ought to make you sleepless at night to think what you've done. You ought to get down on your knees and pray to God to be forgiven. If you aint got a conscience, then make yourselves one. That's a lot better than not having any at all. Everybody ought to have a conscience to tell him when he does something sinful. I've got one, and I'm proud of it. I'd squeeze the heart out of the man or devil who tried to take it away from me. It's the old devil himself who tries to make you ashamed of having one."

The women listened intently. Semon had not yet told them what it was he was preaching about, but they all knew it was something that would interest them. They waited breathlessly for him to say what it was.

"Some folks say only a fool believes in God. I'm a fool about God. Whose fool are you?"

Semon had been preaching for an hour or longer, and he showed no sign of coming to an end. The longer he talked, the louder he shouted; and the harder he pounded the rickety table, the more interested the girls and women became. Some of them who had crying babies hesitated before leaving the room, and they tried their best to quiet the children until Semon finally came out with what he was talking about.

He stopped and breathed deeply.

"Praise God!" he said hoarsely.

The women relaxed for a moment, long enough to glance knowingly at their neighbors.

Semon took off his coat and hung it on the back of a chair. It was hot in the schoolhouse. Outside in the sun the waves of heat extended from the earth as high as some of the treetops, and in the shade it was almost as unbearable. The women fanned themselves with palmleaf fans and with handkerchiefs. The flies swarmed overhead in monotonous circles, coming down in lazy jumps to light on the babies.

Flies and June bugs came in and went out the open doors and

windows at will, and in the four corners of the room gray hornets' bags hung precariously. Dotting the walls and ceiling were yellow crusts of clay around which swarmed mud-daubers. At almost regular intervals a woman would slap her leg with a desperate lunge, jerk her dress above her knees, and flick off a red ant that had stung her. She would scratch the bite until it was swollen and red, and then wet her finger and rub the stinging mound of poisoned flesh.

"Oh, but it hurts me!" Semon cried. "Yes, it does. It hurts me like a bleeding wound. I can't have any peace while I think about it. I look at all your beautiful faces before me this beautiful Sabbath afternoon—I gaze at the beauty in your hair, in your eyes, in your face, and my heart pains me. I know that underneath all this beauty are sinful souls. I know what you think. I know you can't always keep on the strait and narrow path. I know temptation lies with you in your beautiful arms. I know all about it. That's why it hurts me. And, oh, how it hurts me!

"To think that underneath all those pretty dresses that you spend so much care on washing and starching and ironing, frilling and folding—to think that under there is a black sinful soul that hisses in its wickedness like a poisonous snake! Yes, it hurts me. It nearly kills me to think about it. That's why I'm here this afternoon. I came over here to Georgia to save you before it's too late. The Lord told me how wicked you folks in Rocky Comfort are, and he told me to do all I could to save you from hell. We want you in heaven. We need you there. In heaven we want all the beautiful girls and women now in Georgia. Up there you'll look even prettier than you do down here. Up there you'll shine with the beauty of a clean soul. And it hurts me to think that you are going straight to hell. That's where you're going if you don't change your ways before it's too late. Yes, it hurts me. Oh, how it hurts me!"

Semon stopped and wiped his face with his handkerchief. He had heard a mud-dauber droning somewhere around his head, and he stopped and listened to see how close it was. The mud-dauber whirled around in a circle over his head. Semon moved to the other side of the platform and prayed for it to go away and not sting him.

All of the women down in front of him sat still. They were afraid to move for fear of missing one word. Not yet had he told them what he was preaching about, for, or against. And that one word was anxiously awaited. Several of them put their hands under their skirts and scratched the ant bites without even glancing at the marks. Semon had not even hinted at what he was preaching about. They knew he had a definite sin in mind, but, of so many possible sins, it was not easy to determine which one it was. He had kept them on edge for fear they would miss it when he reached the point in his sermon that explained all they wished to know.

The palmleaf fans waved back and forth in front of fifteen or sixteen faces. There was a dry crackle in the palmleaves that sounded like the wind blowing through a canebrake. Other than that, and the occasional swish of a starched skirt that was hastily jerked upward over ant-stung legs, there was no other sound of disturbance. Outside the room there were many sounds; but no one heard those. All lent their ears to the words of Semon Dye.

Semon had refreshed himself sufficiently to continue from where he had stopped a few minutes before. He did not hear the drone of the mud-dauber over his head any longer, and he felt more at ease. He picked up the thread of his sermon and began speaking in a low, almost indistinct voice. The women and girls stopped fanning with the palmleaves for fear they would miss what he was going to say.

Out under the trees, in the circle in the grove, the men sat and looked at each other. There was a hoarse hum in the air when half of them were talking at the same time.

The sun was already sinking behind the trees. It was a little cooler than it had been immediately following midday, when most of them had arrived, and it was no longer necessary to wipe the perspiration away.

Somebody turned around and looked towards the schoolhouse. The man next to Clay nudged him with his elbow.

"Aint that the preacher himself coming out the door, Clay?"

Clay stood up to see better.

"I reckon it must be."

Semon was walking towards the grove, calling Clay.

"Just a minute, Horey," he said sharply. "I'd like to see you just a minute."

He began beckoning to Clay with his hand, urging him to hurry, and waited where he was. When Clay had gone a dozen steps, he called him again.

"I'd like to have a word with Tom Rhodes, too."

"He wants you, too, Tom," Clay said. "You'd better come along and see what's on his mind."

Tom got up and left the circle.

"Don't let the preacher get you into no devilment, Tom," Ralph Stone said.

Everybody in the circle laughed.

"It takes a preacher to think up mischief," somebody said. "I guess they're all alike. I used to know a traveling preacher who was a regular devil."

Clay and Tom walked towards Semon in the school yard. He was pacing up and down with his hands locked behind him as though in deep thought. He did not notice them until they were standing beside him.

"What's the matter, preacher?" Tom said.

"I appoint you and Horey, there, as deacons," Semon said sternly. "That's a trust you mustn't let go of."

"What'll we have to do?" Tom asked. "I aint used to such a thing as that."

"Deacons take up the collections and see that the money is taken care of till it's handed over to me."

"You figure on taking in some money here?"

"I am, I am," Semon replied firmly. "Christians always pay up the preacher."

"You don't know Rocky Comfort folks very well, then," Tom said. "That's what the last preacher who stopped here complained of the most. There aint many around here who's got money to give away."

"Oh, they'll put money in the collection, all right," Semon

assured him. "People are always liberal with the preacher. I always see to that."

"How do you aim for me and Tom to go about getting it?" Clay asked.

"Bring your hats inside and pass them around."

"Oh, that," Clay said. "I know what you mean now. I thought before you spoke that you wanted us to go around prodding folks to give money. I know all about passing the hat around. I've done that before."

"That's fine then," Semon said. "Now, you and Tom come on in behind me, and pass your hats for the money."

He turned and ran up the steps. He did not wait to see if they were following him.

Inside the schoolroom Clay and Tom did not know what to do. They stood there in the back at the door until Semon mounted the platform. He motioned for them to come down to the front.

"Now we'll have the offering," Semon announced. "The deacons will wait on the congregation."

Semon sat down in the chair at the table and waited for Clay and Tom to come down to the first row of desks and begin taking up the collection. When they made no move to come down, Semon motioned to them with his hand. Silently he pointed out to them the first women on each side of the room where they were to start.

Clay went to the corner and held his hat over the woman's lap.

"Put something in the hat," he said.

She shook her head.

"I said, drop something in," he said sharply.

The woman's face turned red, and she shook her head at him.

Clay wheeled around and looked at Semon for further instructions. Semon stared at the woman for a moment, and then nodded to Clay, indicating that he should proceed to the next woman. Over on the other side of the room, Clay could see that Tom was having the same trouble he was having on his side.

He moved to the next woman, looking back at Mrs. Jones until she hung her head in shame.

The hat was held in the correct position, but the second woman made no effort to give. Clay pushed the hat against her bosom, urging her to drop some money into it. She shook her head and looked off into another direction.

"Drop it in," Clay said, shouting at her angrily. "The preacher wants the pay for his preaching."

The woman's face turned red, and she turned around to escape Clay's glare.

"Now, this aint getting nowhere," he said, turning around to look at Semon. "I aint got a penny yet."

Semon was moving around uneasily by that time. He could not sit still on the chair. He got up finally and strode to the edge of the platform and looked over into Clay's black felt hat. He could not see a single coin in it.

"Looks like nobody is going to drop money in my hat," Clay said.

On the other side of the room Tom was finding more response

to Semon's suggestion that he be paid. Tom had two coins in the hat already, and these he jingled by shaking the hat in front of the worshipers. When he came to someone he knew very well, he stopped and said something to her.

It looked to Clay as if there was no use in his going any further. No one had given him so much as a penny yet. He glanced once more at Semon, and Semon nodded to him to go on to the next woman.

Clay shoved his hat under the woman's chin. She turned her head, pretending that she did not see him standing in front of her. That made Clay angry. He slammed his hat against the woman's bosom two or three times in quick succession as though killing a hornet. She looked at him then for the first time, crying out in fright. Clasping her hands tightly around her breasts, she jumped up and fled from the room.

When each woman, girl, and child in the room had been given ample opportunity to contribute, Tom and Clay went to the back near the door and looked into each other's hat. There was nothing in Clay's, but Tom took out several coins. He showed them to Clay and waited to find out what he was expected to do with the money.

He did not have to wait long. Semon called the congregation to its feet and dismissed them with less than half a dozen words. He mumbled the benediction hastily and incoherently, and it was all over before more than half of the women could get to their feet. A moment later he ran down the aisle to the door where Clay and Tom were standing. He pushed them both outside to the school yard.

"How much?" he demanded, reaching for the hats with both hands.

"Twenty cents," Tom said. "I reckon that's all. That's what I took up, and Clay didn't get a cent."

"That's right," Clay said meekly. "I couldn't seem to get anything at all."

Semon shook the money into his hand and looked at the four nickels. He turned them over meditatively several times, and at last he shoved them roughly into his pants pocket.

"I reckon I'll have to do a little heavier preaching tonight," he said. "Looks like it didn't pay this afternoon. I'll bear down on them tonight, though. I reckon I was too easy with them just now."

"That's because the men wasn't in there," Tom said. "Women never have no money, anyway. It's the men who carry what little there is. And the men will all be in there tonight, and you'll have a chance to get what you aimed to take in."

"I reckon that's so," Semon said, nodding. "I'll do my damnedest, anyway. I can't afford to preach for twenty cents."

Chapter XVI

B Y seven that evening no one was ·left outside of the build-ing. Some families had gone home to eat supper, but most of the people had brought supper with them, and they had eaten it in the grove at sundown. Semon had been invited to eat with the Stones, and Clay and Dene and Lorene had stayed.

There was music for the evening service. Homer Johnson was there with his banjo, and Clay played his harmonica. After once starting a hymn, there was little use for Homer and Clay to continue, because the rising flood of song drowned out their efforts. Semon's voice, louder than it had been in the afternoon, could be heard above all the others.

Seven or eight songs and hymns were sung before the sermon began. Semon had announced no text; he merely began preach-ing.

The men sat on the floor because the school desks were not large enough. The women and girls could sit in them comfort-ably, but the others sat on the bare floor and leaned back against the desks.

"I don't want a single man or woman, boy or girl, to leave

this schoolhouse tonight unsaved," Semon told them preliminarily. "I came over here to Georgia to save you, and I aim to do what I set out to do in the start. There's no sense in letting a sinner get away from here tonight—everybody can be saved. It's not easy to be saved; it's a lot harder than going to the devil, but it's easy at that."

Several heads in the audience nodded. A few people in Rocky Comfort considered themselves already saved, and they wished all their neighbors to be denied the pleasures that they themselves had forsworn.

"The devil is on everybody's trail. He dogs a man, day in and day out, sniffing the scent, yelping every once in a while to let you know he's tracking you, and then he slips up on you when you're not looking and grabs you. That's the devil's way of going about his business. You have got to watch out for him. He won't never quit till you stomp him under your heels and beat the life out of him.

"All you old sinners must be the first ones to come over on God's side tonight. That will set the example for the young folks. When a boy or girl's mother and father stand up here and shake my hand, then it won't be long till the sons and daughters come. Now, I want all you old people, all you old sinners, mothers and fathers, to show the way.

"Sin is a bad thing, folks. It saps the life right out of you. I know, because I used to be sinful myself just like all the rest of you. I know what sin is. I've looked it spang in the face. That's why I'm standing here tonight trying to save my brothers and sisters from it. I've seen so many people lose their souls and go to hell, that I can't just sit still and see you folks going there, too. I want to save you. I want to put the devil to shame, so he won't bother you no more. Now, all you men know good and well why you're going to hell when you die, if you don't come over on the Lord's side before it's too late. And tomorrow will be too late. You might die before daybreak tomorrow morning. Nobody ever knows when he's going to do that.

"There's not much use in me telling you why you're going to hell, because you know. You women know why, too. All of you will be smoking in hell if you don't watch out. It don't take much to keep out of there, though. All you have to do is to come over on the Lord's side. It's not too late, but now's the time. Tomorrow might be too late; some of you are going to die soon; if you die in sin, you'll smoke in hell till the world comes to an end, and it may never come to an end.

"All you fornicators and cheaters, all you liars and murderers —all you sinners have got to get sin out of your souls before it's too late. It won't do no good just to stop sinning now; no, that won't do at all. You've got to repent first—you've got to come up here and give me your hand in the presence of the Lord before you can be saved. You men who don't listen to me will wake up after you're dead and smell yourselves smoking in hell— and it'll be too late then. Yes, sir! It will be too late then! Now's the time. It's the only time there'll be for some of you. You might be dead tomorrow, and it'll be too late then to do anything about it. Now's the time!"

Semon stopped for a moment of rest. While he wiped the perspiration from his face, he looked at the faces below him to determine what progress he had made. He noted with pleasure that some of the people were already squirming in their seats on the desks and on the floor.

"Let me tell you a little true story, folks. Away off in a big city there was a young girl. She was as pretty as the day is long. Oh, she was a pretty thing! I've never seen anyone like her since. But that's not it. What I'm telling you is that this pretty girl off in that big city thought she didn't have to heed the call of the Lord. She thought she didn't have to worry about being saved. So she went out one night with a man who came to see her. They rode off in his fine automobile with silver trimming on the doors. They hadn't gone far before the man asked her to take a little drink. She did. She drank the vile stuff. Then they rode some more. She thought she could get by without being saved. So she went riding away in the night. Then they stopped and took another drink of the vile stuff. You know how it is—you keep on and on and can't stop. Then she let the man put his arms around her pure young body. She didn't care about being saved. Oh, no! She thought she didn't have to! So she let him fondle her some. You know how it is—you keep on and on. So he fondled her some. They took another drink of that vile stuff. Then they got out of the car and walked out in the woods— this pure young girl who wouldn't listen to the call of the Lord. Yes, she did! Out there in the dark nobody could see them. But God saw them. Yes, sir, God saw them. Don't ever think you can hide from Him. But He wasn't the only one who saw them. It was the devil. Yes, sir, the devil! The devil came running. He was away off somewhere else when he saw them, but he came running. That's the way he does. And he got there just in time. He got there just in time to tell the man to put his arms around this pure young girl out there in the dark woods. The man stretched her out on the pine needles, and the devil was right there behind him. The devil said: 'Go ahead.' That's what the devil told him. Then he leaned over and told this young girl the same thing. He told her to go ahead, too. And so she said: 'All right.' Yes, sir, that's what she said. She said: 'All right.' So the man got down on the pine needles beside her. Yes, sir. He got right down in the dark——"

"Amen!" somebody said.

Semon stopped abruptly and scrutinized the faces that were all looking at him. He was glad to have a chance to catch his breath, and he liked to hear people utter "Amen" when he was preaching. It was a sign that he had got the people interested.

He wiped his face and continued.

"And so there they were, out there in those dark woods, with the devil standing over them telling them to go ahead. He wanted them to be just as bad as ever they could be. That's his job. It's to make people want to be bad. So he stood right there over them urging them to be bad. And the pure young girl thought she didn't have to listen to the Lord. She thought she could go ahead without Him. Oh, she was so pure! But she thought she could do as she pleased and not listen to God. So she let the man get down beside her. It was in the summertime, and it wasn't cold a bit. Then the devil whispered something else in her ear. Yes, he did! He told her to keep right on where she was headed. So she did. She let the man spoil her right there in the woods. She tried to be spoiled. She had heard the devil, and he had told her to do that nasty thing. She thought she could be saved and not have to bother about keeping her pure young body pure. But she couldn't. After she got up from there, with the mark of the man on her, she was damned. The devil had her. Yes, sir! The devil had her just where he wanted her. She was a little drunk off of that vile stuff, and she had the mark of the man on her. I wish you could have been there to see her walk out of those woods. She wasn't——"

"Amen!"

"She wasn't the same pure young girl who went in there. No, sir! She didn't look the same. She was laughing. She was having a good time. She felt good. She had the mark of the man on her! She had her arms around the man's waist, and she jumped up and down, she felt so good. She came skipping out of there and got back into the automobile, and the mark of the man was on her. The devil had got in his work for the night, all right, all right. Yes, sir! The mark of the man was on that young girl. He had her just where he——"

"Amen!" somebody shouted again.

Semon stopped and took off his coat. It was getting hot in the schoolhouse. The air was thick, and there was no motion in it. It hung in the room, pressing down on skulls and chests, and got hotter and hotter.

"Now, who's going to be the first to come up here and give himself to the Lord?"

People in the room turned and craned their necks in all directions. Everyone looked to see who would be the first to go up and grasp Semon's hand.

"I'm waiting to clasp the hand of those who want to be saved. That's what I'm here for. I came here to save men and women. If you want to be saved, come up here and shake me by the hand. If you have got the devil in you, if he's telling you to stay in your seat, if he's whispering in your ear to tell you to keep on cheating people out of money—if he's trying to do that, then get up and wrestle with him. Throw him down and kick the stuffing out of him. You men out there—you men who are slipping out every once in a while to visit a darky girl behind the barn—you men get together and fight the devil. And you women and girls—you women and girls who slip out to meet men at night—you fornicating women who have got the mark of the man on you—get together and scratch the eyes out of the devil. He'll run! He always runs when you scrap him. He can't stand up and fight back. He aint man enough. So go ahead and fight the devil, folks—all you sinning men and women. I don't want to miss you folks in heaven when I get there. I'd hate to go there and not see all you people there. I'd hate that. Yes, sir! I'd sure enough hate that."

No one moved. Semon waited a while, wiping his face.

"We'll have a little singing while you're coming up to the front," he said. "Horey, you and Homer strike up a tune."

As soon as the singing started, some of the men stood up and stretched their arms and backs. Soon everyone had joined in the hymn.

"Now, come on!" Semon shouted above the voices of the singers. "Don't be scared. The Lord will help you. Come on up here and take your stand with me and God. Come on up here and put the devil to shame. You women and girls sitting out there with the mark of the man on you—you folks come on up here and be saved!"

Semon stepped down from the platform and walked to the nearest desk. He leaned over and whispered something in a woman's ear. She looked embarrassed.

Chapter XVII

YES, you want to be saved," Semon told her aloud. "God wants you to be saved. He needs fine-looking women like you in heaven. Don't sit there and help the devil out by going to hell when you die. Let's help God line up the prettiest women in Georgia. Don't let the devil have you down there in the other place."

The woman hung back for a while, but when Semon took her arm and pulled her forward, she gladly allowed herself to be led to the bench in front of the platform.

Semon went next to a man.

"You aint going to let a woman put you to shame, are you, coz? A man ought to be braver than a woman. Now, come on up and cast yourself on the side of the Lord."

"I can't accommodate you, preacher," the man said. "I just sure enough can't."

"You just think you can't. But you can. And you want to. You don't think it's important, but just you wait till judgment day! And then it will be too late. When the devil comes to carry you off with him, you'll yell and kick and wish you had listened to me."

"I aint never done much meanness, preacher," the man protested.

"Oh, yes, you have, coz! You've been as mean as an old snake! You forget it now, but you'll be reminded of it on judgment day."

"It won't cost me nothing to go up there, will it?"

"Just a handshake," Semon said, leading him to the bench and pushing him down close to the woman.

He went for another woman to place beside the man.

The hymn was being sung for the third time. Clay and Homer were playing with all their might.

Somebody screamed in the middle of the room. Semon stopped talking to the woman and ran to see about it. The revival was progressing faster than he had realized. He knew then that he would be able to dispense with the mourners' bench and plunge headlong into exhortation of sinners.

It was Lucy Nixon who had screamed. She was the first to have the spirit move her.

"God be praised!" Semon said, rubbing his hands together.

Lucy continued to shake violently, her body quivering all over. Semon took her by the arm and led her down the aisle to the platform.

"She's coming through!" he shouted to the people.

Lucy's hair had fallen down, and her face was distorted. Each time she screamed, she jumped higher into the air.

"God be praised!" he shouted. "She's coming through!"

The men who had congregated in the rear of the room pushed forward in a mass. Everybody had to see the Nixon girl shake herself.

Semon left her for a moment to go down on a level with the people. He wished to bring others to the front bench while the excitement was on. The girl was screaming at regular intervals. When she grew too weak to leap into the air, she began hitting herself with her fists. She pounded her body, leaving red marks on her arms and face.

"Praise God!" a man shouted. He leaped high into the air, pulling his hair and making unintelligible sounds in his throat.

Lucy Nixon became more convulsive.

"She's coming through!" Semon yelled, running back to the platform. He stood beside her ready to catch her if she should suddenly go under.

"Yeeee yow!" somebody in another part of the room yelled.

"Praise the Lord!" Semon said, turning to look at the man. "The devil is leaving another sinner!"

"Amen!"

Lucy began tearing her clothes. She ripped the sleeves from her dress, and began pulling the dress from her and hurling the pieces of torn cloth into the air. The people crowded forward, pushing and shoving each other out of the way. All over the room there were screams and shouts. Some of the women had already fallen on the floor and were writhing under the desks in the dust. No one paid any attention to them then. Everyone was trying to see Lucy Nixon come through.

"Praise God!" Semon shouted.

"Amen!" a man yelled.

"Yeeee-yow!" another man cried.

"Amen!" a woman said, half screaming. She immediately fell on the floor, kicking and moaning. No one noticed her again.

Lucy screamed as though she were being murdered. The scream filled the room and tore at the straining ear-drums of the closely packed, perspiring people. Her hair had fallen all around her head, and she jerked and flung it out of her eyes. She shook convulsively all over again, and the hair fell to blind her once more. She was still standing. Others who had been seized with the desire to come through had fallen on the floor. But Semon waited beside her so he could keep her standing in full view as long as possible. Everything Lucy wore had been torn. The men pushed forward to stare and rub their legs together. There were still a few who had not been seized with a desire to come through.

Semon hovered around the girl, ready to catch her if she should fall. She was having a terrific struggle. She was in painful, labor. Most of the others who had been seized had immediately passed into a state of helplessness, falling semi-consciously to the floor to lie there and squirm under the desks in the dust. But Lucy was having a more difficult time of it. She could not quite come through. She beat herself, ripped her skin with her finger-nails, screaming each time she drew breath, and all the time her body shook and trembled with jerky muscular contortions.

One of the women on the bench in front of the platform leaped two feet into the air, pulling at her clothes and screaming at the top of her lungs. She fell on the floor at Semon's feet, tearing her clothes from her body and jerking her lower limbs as in the death-agony of a knife-stuck hog; no one looked at her after she had fallen.

Up on the platform Lucy Nixon had been standing for fifteen or twenty minutes, and she still could not make herself come through. Her body trembled all over. She would become motionless for a moment, and then her shoulders would begin to shake. The trembling would gradually grow in intensity until her whole body was shaking. Then she would become still again. Soon her stomach would begin to undulate. She would hold herself rigidly stiff, gripping her hands above her head until the veins in her arms looked like lines of black ink; but even then her stomach would move with an undulating motion, backward and forward, up and down.

A man who had pushed forward until he was on the platform hurled himself against the wall and began squirming against it in a circular motion. His grunts and movements became more frantic each second.

"Praise God!" Semon shouted. "Bring this girl through!"

"Amen!" somebody shouted at the top of his voice.

"Yeeee-yow!" The yell shook the walls of the frame building.

"Praise God!"

Lucy's body was inflamed with exertion. Her skin was hot and damp, and blood ran from her mouth where she had bitten her lips. But she had not come through even then. Her body still trembled, not all at once any longer, but first her shoulders, next her breasts, then her stomach, and finally her thighs. Her hips and buttocks were in violent agitation again. Her thighs moved up and down, to the right and to the left, and then in all directions. The motions she made sent screams and yells ringing through the timbers of the building. Men were prancing up and down like unruly stallions, and women shook themselves in time with her movements. A man who had been watching her for several minutes suddenly grasped the fly of his breeches with his fist and ran yelling into the crowd. Bursting buttons flew into the air like spit-balls. Semon had gone closer to Lucy, almost touching her, and he bent forward to watch her labor.

"Praise God!"

"Amen! Amen!"

"Yeeee-yow!"

"Praise God!"

Tom Rhodes was on the floor. He was dirty all over, and his clothes were stuck to his body with perspiration. He rolled into a corner, hitting himself against the wall with clock-like regularity. Just behind him was Dene on the floor. She had just started. She was a long way from coming through, but she was determined.

Lucy Nixon's frenzy had slowed down. She was almost too weak to keep it up any longer. She had not come through, and she was as troubled as some of the others who had not yet even been seized with the desire. She had become pale, and her arms hung at her sides; but she continued to labor with her body. Semon expected her to fall at almost any second. He was ready to catch her so she would not be hurt.

The music had long since died out. Clay remained seated in

the chair where he had been playing the harmonica, but there was a look on his face that showed plainly that he would soon be seized. Homer, beside him, continued to pluck the strings of the banjo. He was not playing a tune, however; and the chords he struck were hurled back at him by the upheaval in the room.

During a lull in the deafening noise, Semon, who had been watching her closely, stepped forward and caught Lucy in his arms. She was completely exhausted, and she could not stand any longer. Even her eyelids did not move. Semon held her limp body in his arms, looking down at her and pushing away with his hips the crowding men who tried to get to her. Finally he succeeded in kicking several so savagely that they kept at a distance.

Semon laid her on the table and grabbed a palmleaf fan from somebody and began trying to revive her. She had to be revived so she could come through.

Chapter XVIII

THERE were only four or five persons left standing or sitting by that time. Everyone else was rolling on the floor in the dust and dirt, struggling under a desk, or beating himself with his fists.

Semon left Lucy in order to help the ones who had not yet been seized with the desire to come through. He went first to Clay.

"Praise God!" he said.

"I feel it in my bones," Clay apologized, "but I can't get it to act."

"Get down on your knees and pray for it, Horey!" Semon ordered him. "Get down and do your damnedest to come through."

"Will that help?"

"Get down and do it, coz. It may be too late next time. Now's the time to get religion if you're ever going to get it. Pray, coz!"

Clay got down on his knees beside the chair, resting his head on his arms, and wondered how he could make himself do it.

"I've got to get religion," he cried. "Dene's getting it, and everybody else's getting it. I'll be the only sinner left in Rocky Comfort if I don't get it."

Just then Semon thought of Lorene. He had not seen her anywhere since the meeting began.

He turned around, walking off, and searched for her. She was sitting behind a desk near the center of the room, watching the actions of the people. She showed no sign of coming through. Semon knew by the expression on her face that she was not even trying.

He ran to her, leaping over prostrate figures on the floor.

"What's the matter, Lorene?" he asked her.

"Nothing," she replied.

"Can't you get it?"

"Get what?"

"Religion, Lorene!"

"I don't want it," she said.

"Praise God!" Semon cried. His face was flushed, his eyes were ablaze, and his body was tense with excitement.

She looked upon him with no concern.

"Praise God!" he said again, louder. He was too excited to speak. He could not believe that Lorene had not caught the desire to come through that had gripped everybody else in the building.

He dropped to his knees beside her, holding one of her hands in his, and began praying aloud for her.

After several sentences he looked up to see if his efforts had had any effect on her. She looked at him a little queerly for a moment.

"What do you want me to do?" she said. "I don't know how to do it."

"Praise God!" he shouted, jumping to his feet. "Come through, Lorene! Praise God, come through!"

"How do you do it?"

"Give yourself to God, Lorene. Praise God! Just give yourself to God!"

Semon began jumping up and down in front of her. He made unintelligible sounds in his throat. He pulled at her arms.

"Unga-unga! Praise God!"

Clay ran up and down the room, jumping and leaping over writhing bodies on the floor. His shirt had been torn off, and his pants were held in place by only one suspender strap.

"I've got it!" he yelled. "I've got it!"

Semon dropped Lorene's hand and ran to be near Clay.

"Got what, Horey!"

"Got religion, man!"

"How much have you got it?"

"I'm coming through!"

"Praise God!" Semon yelled.

Clay ran around the room leaping over the prostrate bodies on the floor. He narrowly missed jumping on to the heads of several people. He ran up and down, waving his arms over his head.

"I've got it!"

"What's the matter, Clay?" somebody yelled, clutching at his arm as he ran past. He jerked free and did not stop to see who it was.

"I've got it!"

"Praise God!" Semon cried, running after him.

"I'm coming through!"

Over in a corner alone Dene was laboring in the first pain of coming through. She did not take up as much space as some of the others, and she did not get in other people's way. She stayed by herself, rolling and hitting her head against the wall occasionally.

Clay tore around the room as though a wild-cat were after him.

"I've got it!" he yelled again, leaping over desks and jumping over bodies.

"Got what, Horey?" Semon said, catching his arm and trying his best to hold him.

"I've got religion! I've got it!"

Clay fell headlong on the floor, kicking and yelling. Semon turned away to give his attention to someone else who needed his help to come through.

He thought of Lorene sitting stiffly upright at her desk. He ran back to where she was.

When he dropped on his knees at her side, she looked at him as though she thought he was completely crazy.

"Lorene," he begged, "try to come through for me now, won't you? Nearly everybody else in the schoolhouse has come through except you. I don't want to see a single sinner left unsaved to-night. This might be the last chance for Rocky Comfort."

Lorene looked at him without answering.

"Praise God!" he said.

Catching her hand, he again began making unintelligible sounds in his throat. The perspiration broke out on his forehead and face, and ran down in streams to his shirt. His hands were gripped tightly around hers, and his face was twisted and contorted.

"Praise God!" he said again.

Lorene watched him on his knees beside the desk where she sat. She felt sorry for him at one moment; the next moment she could not help laughing at him. His body was swaying, and grunts and groans broke from his tightly compressed lips. He was doing his best to make her come through, but she remained unmoved.

Semon's face was red and wet.

"Unga-unga!" she thought he said.

A woman had rolled against him and was struggling at his side. He paid no attention to her. He continued to exhort Lorene, making sounds in his throat that she could not understand.

"Unga-unga!"

She felt like telling Semon he was wasting his time but she hated to disturb him. He looked then as if he were happy. His face was losing its expression of pain, and a beatific smile spread over his face. A moment later he was sprawling on the floor, writhing and kicking and tearing his hair and clothes. He lay on the floor in the dirt and dust at her feet, kicking his lower limbs as though each successive movement would be his last on earth.

Some of the others crowded around Semon, and Lorene had to raise her feet and sit on them in order to keep her legs from being broken. The men and women wrenching on the floor under her muttered meaningless sounds that beat against her ears like the memory of a screaming nightmare.

After a while Semon became still. A woman raised his head and held it on her lap while she fanned him with a splintered palmleaf. When he opened his eyes, the first thing he saw was Lorene sitting above him, scoffing.

He was on his feet in a second. He stood looking down at Lorene while perspiration once more rolled from his face and forehead. He could say nothing for a while.

It was then that he realized that he had failed to bring Lorene through. He had never failed before in all his life. That was what troubled him.

"Praise God!" he said weakly.

He had tried so hard to make Lorene come through that he had come through himself. Lorene, the woman whom he thought the worst sinner in the schoolhouse, had ridiculed his efforts and had laughed at him. He had failed utterly.

Even though he realized his failure, he felt that he could not let himself down then. He was determined to bring the meeting to a successful close.

He ran to the platform where Lucy Nixon lay on the table.

"Praise God!"

"Amen!" somebody said.

Almost all the people had already come through, and those

who were on their feet crowded around Semon. Semon noticed that Tom Rhodes was still struggling on the floor. He prodded Tom with his foot.

"Yeeee-yow!" Tom yelled. His voice, like a hoarse bullfrog's, could be recognized in any crowd.

Semon laid his hand on Lucy's wrist to feel her pulse. He began fanning her again with the palmleaf fan, and murmuring unintelligibly to himself.

"Praise God!"

Semon looked down on the floor in front of the platform and saw several men and women, torn and dirty, struggling in a mass. They were moaning and kicking, and every once in a while one of them gave a gigantic jerk that looked as if it could wrench a body apart.

Lucy was breathing more deeply by then, and Semon continued to fan her. As far as he knew, she was the only person in the schoolhouse, except Lorene, who had not come through.

"Praise God!" he said, looking at her closely. She had opened her eyes.

Fully two thirds of the men and women had become silent and still, though most of them still lay on the floor. All of them were dust-covered and damp, but on their faces were smiles of contented pleasure.

"Praise God!" Semon shouted at Lucy.

She moved her arm and tried to get up. Semon lifted her to a sitting position on the table. All at once she became alive again. It was as if her strength had held itself back in anticipation of that moment. She leaped from the table to the platform and ran leaping up and down from one wall to the other. Semon ran after her, never catching up with her, but trying to help her come through this time.

Her screams seemed to have awakened everyone else in the room. For, a moment later, the people who had been either lying still or jerking feebly, at the sound of her voice squirmed and wriggled like a nest of snakes in a dry well.

Lucy stopped at last and stood still. Her head was thrown back and her hands gripped tightly across her stomach. Her body shook, swiftly and convulsively, and she began shaking herself again.

"Praise the Lord!" Semon shouted.

"Yeeee-yow!" a man under a desk yelled. It sounded like Tom Rhodes.

Lucy Nixon began to scream with each expulsion of her breath. It was a sound that sent shivers up backbones that were almost too worn and tired to respond to further stimulation. The thrusting forward, backward, and sideways of her thighs made her breath come short. Her screams came at shorter intervals, but they were louder than they had ever been before.

Semon could see the women in the mass in front of the platform squirm with renewed vigor. Most of them had their legs locked around the legs of the desks, and the men lay flat on their stomachs moving and twisting.

He watched Lucy in her frantic struggle to come through.

The others around them were trying to help her. They pushed closer to her, yelling and screaming with her, and rubbing against each other. Some of them stood apart and began going through a duplication of her motions, trying in that way to help her.

When it seemed as if the arteries in her body would burst through her skin, Lucy's face became less distorted and her motions more intense. She began to smile a little, and the tension of her muscles drew knots to her legs and arms. After that she gradually relaxed, slowly, in jerking rapture.

"Praise God!" somebody shouted.

There was then an expression of bliss on Lucy's face that grew with the passing of each second. At last, with a final effort, she did come through; and the evidence was there to show that she had. While everybody stared, someone covered her thighs with a coat; but by that time everyone had seen what had happened.

While the men crowded closer to see, her motions became slower and slower, and finally she lay perfectly still. Not even an eyelid moved.

When it was all over, Semon sank exhausted in a heap on the floor. He felt his legs giving away under him, and he could not stop himself. When he realized that he had fallen on the floor, he made no immediate effort to rise. The people who were close to him thought he was coming through for the second time, and they turned away to allow him to be alone. He was tired to the core of his body.

Everyone had become quiet, and there was only the sound of people walking on the floor. When anything was said, it was spoken in low whispers.

Lucy's family had come forward and carried her out of the schoolhouse. She was laid in the wagon-bed and covered with those pieces of her clothing that could be found. She lay in the wagon-bed staring at the heavens through the waving branches of the pines while her mother and father and brothers were getting ready to leave.

No one spoke coming out of the schoolhouse. People walked silently on the thick carpet of pine needles towards their wagons and cars.

Clay got into the automobile alone. Soon Dene came and sat down beside him, and Lorene followed. They waited for Semon in silence.

Back in the schoolhouse Semon got up and took several steps. He found that he was too exhausted to move. He sat down at a desk, holding his head in his hands. He felt sick and discouraged. He had saved perhaps forty people that night; but the most hardened sinner he could not help. Lorene had sat through the meeting unmoved and, in the end, unsaved.

Semon got up and started blowing out the smoking lamps. It was then, when he was ready to leave the building, that he remembered that he had forgotten to take up the collection. He left the darkened building with dragging feet.

On the way home they passed several wagons of people, and two or three men walking, and several on mule-back. The horn was not sounded, and the only thing that could be heard was the hum of the motor and the clanking of trace-chains on the wagons. They passed on ahead and were soon out of sight.

Chapter XIX

C LAY was unaccustomed to being up late at night, and the sun was two hours high when he opened his eyes. He lay on his side, batting his eyes bewilderedly, and wondered why he had overslept. Springing to the floor, he remembered that it had been after midnight when they got home from the schoolhouse.

No one else was to be heard. Dene was sound asleep on her side of the bed, and she looked so exalted that he did not wake her. He slipped on his shirt and overalls, tied his shoelaces, and went out on the back porch to get a drink of water.

He knew at the instant he went to the railing and dipped some water from the bucket that everything was not as it should have been. At first he could not determine what the trouble was. He scanned as much of the yard as he could with a sweep of his eyes, and ran down the steps towards the barn trying to find out what it was that had told him something was wrong.

"I'll be doggone," he said, staring at the shed.

The car that had always stood under the shed beside the barn was not there. He remembered distinctly that it had been driven under the shed the night before. But now it was not there.

He turned and ran around the corner of the house. Without pausing to look closely, he could see fresh tire tracks on the sand. There had been a shower of rain some time between midnight and daybreak, and the new tracks on the sand were as clear and distinct as footprints in newly laid concrete. Clay went as far as the front yard, and there he stopped.

"I'll be doggone, if I won't," he muttered, looking down the big road towards McGuffin.

Slowly he turned and dragged himself to the front steps. His body bending, he sank to the next to the bottom tread. His arms lay extended over his sharp knees, his elbows bending, and they hung half suspended there.

Down at the cabins Hardy came out of his kitchen door, his right arm in a sling around his neck, and walked to the woodpile. He bent down and picked up chips, tossing them into a handleless bucket.

Semon's old car still stood under the magnolia tree in front of the house. It had not been moved an inch since the day Semon had arrived. From where Clay sat on the steps he could see that three of the tires were flat, and that the fourth one would soon be down.

There was behind him in the house a muffled stir. He supposed it was Dene getting up to cook breakfast. He made no effort to stop her; Sugar was back, and she could come to the house to cook, but Clay remained silent and allowed nothing to disturb him.

Hearing a step in the hall behind him, he turned around to tell Dene that Sugar and Hardy had come back. But when he looked, he saw Lorene instead. She was dressed in the clothes she had worn when she came several days before, and she had on her hat. She even had her handbag with her.

"You aint leaving, are you, Lorene?" he said.

"Where is he?" she asked, running out on the porch.

"Where's who?"

"Semon."

Clay turned around in order to see her better.

"Well, I'll be doggone!" he said. "Did you get up to go off with him?"

She nodded, running to the steps and looking in'all directions for Semon.

"You might just as well go back in the house and eat breakfast," he said, "becáuse Semon Dye's more than likely twenty miles on the other side of McGuffin by this time. He made away with an early start."

Lorene dropped her handbag to the porch.

"The low-down son of a bitch," she said, speaking through flat lips. "He told me he'd take me back to Jacksonville with him."

"He did?" Clay said. "Well, I'll be doggone!"

Lorene sat down in a chair, glaring down the road in the direction Semon had gone sometime during the night. She took off her hat, flinging it to the porch floor.

She was saying something inaudible through clenched teeth.

"I reckon I could call him some names, too," Clay told her, "if I only knew what to say. It was a dirty shame for him to go off like that, leaving everybody high and dry like this."

They both sat silent for a while, each looking down the road towards McGuffin. Clay felt weak over the loss of his car, but he would not have felt so badly if Semon had not gone away as he had. He had hoped to have the satisfaction of seeing Semon drive out of the yard and out of sight down the road. He felt cheated now.

While they were sitting there, Dene ran out on the porch. She did not see either of them until she was almost at the steps. When she saw Clay and Lorene, she stopped quickly.

"What's—!"

She could not finish. She stepped backward.

"What makes you so wild-eyed, Dene?" Clay said, looking at her closely. "You act like the house was on fire."

Dene was not dressed for travel, but she had on her best slippers and her new frock.

"I'll be doggone if you don't look like you don't know what to do, Dene," he said.

He saw her glance quickly at Lorene and at the hat on the floor.

"Lorene was aiming to ride back to Jacksonville with Semon, but Semon hot-footed it away and left her behind."

"Has Semon left, sure enough?" Dene asked excitedly.

Lorene shrugged her shoulders and cursed under her breath. She gave no other reply to Dene's question.

"It don't look like you folks ought to be so wrought up about Semon going off," Clay said, "because he didn't take nothing that belonged to you. Looks like I ought to be the one to do all the swearing at him. Semon rode off in my automobile. I reckon maybe he had a right to it, but it don't look like he'd ride off in the night. He could act like a white man about it. I wasn't aiming to stop him. I just wanted to see him go."

Dene sat down on the edge of a chair and gazed down the road towards McGuffin. After several minutes she glanced hurriedly at Lorene once more. Lorene looked at no one; she stared grimly at the porch floor.

A smile passed over Clay's face.

"Semon didn't tell you he'd take you with him, too, did he, Dene?"

A moment later he turned and glared angrily at the ground in front of him.

"By God," he said to himself, "I never thought of that before."

Down at Sugar and Hardy's cabin the blind at the kitchen window was thrown open. Sugar could be seen standing in the window looking at the house.

"I reckon I'd better go down and tell Sugar to come and start breakfast," he said. "The sun's way up there in the sky, and I'm getting as hungry as a dog."

He made no effort then to move from the steps.

Behind him he thought he heard a suppressed sob in someone's throat. He did not turn around to see who was crying. He knew it was not Lorene, though; if Lorene was doing anything, she was swearing under her breath.

"Somehow I sort of hate to see Semon go away now and leave us. It makes me feel left high and dry. I'm going to miss having him around here for a while to come. It makes me feel lonesome, not hearing him talk and not seeing him sitting on the porch, waiting for Sunday to come."

He paused for a moment.

"Sunday has come and gone."

A chair scraped on the floor behind him, and someone ran sobbing into the house. He did not turn around to see who it was.

"Semon was a sort of low-down scoundrel, taking all in all, but he had a way with him just the same. I couldn't put up with a rascal like him very long, because I'd sooner or later go get my shotgun and blast away at him. But it does sort of leave a hollow feeling inside of me to know he aint here no longer. I feel left high and dry, like a turtle on its back that can't turn over."

He was not surprised to see a car appear out of the still morning. It was racing down the road, coming from the direction of the schoolhouse. When it got to the cabins where Vearl and the pickaninnies were playing, it slowed down a little.

When the car came closer, he could see Tom Rhodes twisting the steeringwheel from side to side. He did not get up to meet him.

"Up early, Tom," he said. "Something the matter up your way?"

Tom ran up the walk, carrying a gallon jug of his corn whisky.

"Where's the preacher? Aint he up yet?"

"He's up, all right," Clay said.

"I've got something here for him. I thought I'd like to bring him a drink for pulling me through last night in the schoolhouse.

And, too, I thought maybe you and him would like to go back home with me and we could sit in the shed and look through the crack some."

Tom pulled the stopper and offered the jug to Clay. After swallowing several mouthfuls, Clay handed the jug back, wiping his lips with the back of his hand and licking it.

"I hope you aint easily disappointed, Tom," he said. "I got bad news for you."

"What's it about?" Tom asked, drinking from the jug.

"Semon Dye's up and gone, Tom. He pulled up stakes and left before any of us was up. I reckon he's way on the other side of McGuffin by now, headed south. I don't reckon we'll ever see him again this side of heaven—or hell, which's more like it."

"Gone?" Tom said, shaking his head. "You don't mean to say Semon's gone, Clay! Aint the preacher here now!"

"That's right. He's gone."

Tom set the jug heavily on the porch and looked at it. He glanced at Lorene in the chair by the window.

"That makes me feel real sad," he said, sitting down beside Clay. He picked up the jug and held it in his arms. "I feel so sad I don't know what to do about it."

"Maybe me and you could take the jug and go back to your place and sit in the shed," Clay suggested. "I sure would like to sit there once more and look through the crack some. It's one pretty sight for sore eyes."

Tom pulled the stopper and handed the jug to Clay. When it was returned to him, he looked down through the hole at the colorless liquor and blew his breath into it. It made a sound like wind at night blowing through a gourd tied to a fence post.

Clay reached to the ground for a handful of pebbles. He shook them in his hand, sifting the sand through his fingers. When they were free of sand, he took them one by one and shot them across the yard like marbles. Tom watched him, moving his head back and forth each time one of the little round stones was flicked down the path.

Neither of them turned around to look at Lorene when she got up and walked heavily across the porch and into the hall.

"God help the people at the next place Semon picks out to stop and preach," Clay said. He flung the remaining pebbles on the ground. "But I reckon they'll be just as tickled to have him around as I was."

He got up and walked slowly down the path. When he reached the gate, he stopped for a moment to gaze at the old automobile under the shade of the magnolia tree. Then he went down the road through the hot white sand to tell Sugar to come to the house and start breakfast.

THE END